MW01134624

John — I Love Looking Back at our College Days. You were a Big Part of my life!

David

Between Here and There

B. DAVID CISNEROS

ARCHWAY
PUBLISHING

Archway Publishing books may be ordered through booksellers or by contacting:

Archway Publishing
1663 Liberty Drive
Bloomington, IN 47403
www.archwaypublishing.com
844-669-3957

Exterior Image Credit: Sean Ramsey
www.southernplainsphotography.com

ISBN: 978-1-6657-0799-2 (sc)
ISBN: 978-1-6657-0797-8 (hc)
ISBN: 978-1-6657-0798-5 (e)

Library of Congress Control Number: 2021911427

Print information available on the last page.

Archway Publishing rev. date: 10/15/2021

For my children, Ana, Olivia, and Diego. Ana is my middle child, but I listed her name first so I wouldn't forget.

And to everyone who read the early drafts and encouraged me to keep going. Thank you.

CHAPTER 1

He awoke from a strange dream.

Moonlight glowed inside the little boy's bedroom while the stillness of night surrounded him.

Who were they? he wondered while searching for clues of them in the shadows.

He had dreamed about a small gathering with people he'd known and loved, yet he hadn't recognized any of them. He had told them goodbye because he would soon be leaving them all—forever. For some reason, leaving them hadn't bothered him in the dream, though he fought to hold back his tears as he lay hidden underneath his covers.

Don't be sad, the voice inside him said. *You will see them again.*

When? he asked.

Soon, the voice said.

The voice often spoke to the little boy when he was alone and confused. But their conversations were usually short.

I'm you, the voice would explain. But hearing this frightened the little boy.

Before the voice could say more, the little boy did his best to hide from it. *Just go back to sleep*, he told himself. *It was a stupid dream.* He rolled onto his side, closed his eyes, and pulled the covers in tight.

His thoughts turned to the important day ahead and the warning his mother had issued: he'd have to be on his best behavior and wear his best clothes. He didn't want to disappoint her.

Eventually, the little boy drifted back to sleep.

The following afternoon, his family arrived late to his grandmother's house. Strangers were already there and were dressed formally.

The little boy had never seen her house so crowded. Flower arrangements and plates of food were everywhere, and people seemed to be in every room.

His grandmother had but one grandchild, and she'd always given him her undivided attention. But today was different. Today he seemed to be competing for her attention—and he was losing. He decided to stay as close to her as he could to win back what he'd lost. He sat quietly beside her on the beige couch covered in clear plastic. He held her hand.

One after another, the strangers came to visit with his grandmother, and he listened in on what they had to say. He noticed that no matter how long they were with her, she always seemed thoughtful to everyone.

A woman with short gray hair and wearing a dark blue dress was with her now. She smiled at the little boy before addressing his grandmother. He forced a smile back at her but only because he thought he should.

His grandmother then invited her to sit with them. Although he shied away from people he didn't know, he somehow understood that he needed to stay where he was.

The plastic scrunched and squeaked as the woman settled in. While they spoke, the little boy kept a careful watch on his parents, who were standing in a corner not far away. His mother seemed upset—he could tell by the way she was yelling at his father in a whispering voice and pressing him against a tall glass shelf. The little boy grew concerned that the shelf would tip over, and his grandmother's prized pink-flower teacups and plates would crash to the ground.

As he watched their every move, he sensed the strangers watching them too. He wanted to hide from the embarrassment of his mother's voice growing louder and louder. But he had nowhere to go. He wondered what his father had done this time to upset her. *It could be anything,* he thought, and he crossed his fingers and hoped his father would just apologize so it would end.

A short time later, the woman in the dark blue dress stood to say goodbye. He saw her press her lips tightly together, and she held them that way as she walked away. She wasn't smiling, he could see, but she wasn't frowning either. He wondered what she was thinking about.

Suddenly, his mother let out a shout. "You're such an idiot!"

He turned to see her sticking her finger into his father's chest. Just as the little boy feared, his father backed into the shelf and nearly knocked it over. His father struggled to keep everything from falling. His mother just watched him. She had on a peculiar smile, as if she were amused. She turned and left him there, and his father eventually chased after her down the hall.

The little boy drew in a deep breath.

"Everything will be just fine," his grandmother whispered to him while she caressed his hand.

A quiet moment later, the little boy asked his grandmother the question he'd been holding for as long as he could remember. "G-Grandma?" he said in his gentle, stuttering voice.

"Yes?"

"Why d-do we d-die?"

"Well, it's just our time to go," she answered.

"B-But why?"

"Only God knows the answer to that."

"B-But why does G-God want us to d-die?" the little boy asked.

"He doesn't want us to die," she said. "God just wants us to return home. So that we can be with him again."

"We used to l-l-live with G-God?" he asked, imagining what the house looked like and the things inside.

"Well, of course we did," said his grandmother.

As she assured him, he became drawn into her crystal-green eyes. "I d-don't remember d-doing that," he said.

"Not many of us can," she said.

The little boy turned from her to look out the front window. There he spotted a small orange fruit tree in the front yard. He focused on it while trying his hardest to recall even the slightest memory of living with God and imagining what he looked like. A whisper of last night's dream then came to him but vanished as quickly as it had arrived.

"I d-don't want to g-go there, Grandma," he said quickly. "And I d-don't want you to g-go either."

"I'm sorry, but it's not our choice—it's God's." She paused, seeming to hold back tears. "I wish we all had more time here. But when he calls for us, we have to go."

"We g-go back to heaven?" he asked.

"Yes."

"Wh-What's there?"

Before she could answer him, an older couple approached. The tall, skinny man was dressed in a dark suit and a black tie, and the plump woman wore a flowy black dress.

"Can I get you anything?" the man asked his grandmother.

"Oh no. I'm fine," she answered. "But thank you."

"I thought the service was just beautiful," the woman said. "I think he would've loved it."

"I think so too," his grandmother said.

The three of them spoke for several more minutes, but the little boy hardly heard a word.

I want to know what God does in heaven, he thought. *And I want to know what people do there too.* Suddenly, another feeling from last night's dream came to him. He didn't know why, but returning to heaven didn't seem so bad after all.

He sat quietly and pondered while waiting for the older couple to leave. But the little boy's innocent curiosity quickly turned to angst when he heard his mother's raspy voice grow louder down the hall.

"I'm so done with you!" his mother shouted.

He looked up to see her enter the living room with his father close behind. They went back to the empty corner with the glass shelf, but his father stood farther away from the shelf this time. All the strangers in the room, he noticed, had stopped what they were doing to stare at them.

The little boy felt his hand being squeezed again as the older couple said their goodbyes to his grandmother and walked away.

"Everything will be just fine," she whispered to him once more. "And don't you worry about a thing. Don't worry."

The little boy scrunched his lips together while he watched and listened. It was the same way the old woman in the blue dress had pursed her lips minutes earlier, though he didn't realize he was doing it.

His mother shouted one last thing at his father before hurrying toward the little boy.

"G-G-Grandma?" he said quietly, quivering.

"Don't worry." She tried to reassure him as she nudged him closer.

He wanted to trust her—he really did—but he knew what was to come. His mother got to him quickly, and she stood over him with her arms crossed and her nostrils flared. She blathered something to his grandmother, saying things the little boy knew she shouldn't have, especially on a day like today.

"Everything's fine. I promise," his grandmother told her.

But his mother disagreed with a heavy scowl. Then, without warning, she grabbed his arm and started pulling him toward the front door. He looked back to see his grandmother pleading with her to stay, but that just made his mother move faster, hurting his arm even more. He didn't check to see, but he knew the eyes of the strangers were glued to him now.

Not long after, the little boy was alone in the backseat of the family car and looking out the passenger-side window. He spotted the orange fruit tree, and he kept his eye on it as it steadily grew smaller and smaller.

CHAPTER 2

The little boy's name was Raymond, and his parents were Evelyn and Clay. The Boyd family lived in a tired two-bedroom house in a dusty farming town in Central California.

Ray's father owned a small welding shop and repaired equipment for the local farmers. Every day, Clay tried his hardest to show Ray what a hard worker looked like, always leaving for work early in the morning and returning home late at night. Some mornings, Ray would find his father sleeping in the living room on his worn-out recliner with his work clothes and the television still on.

On the other hand, Ray's mother taught him what it was like to be an irresponsible mess. She'd often brag about the incredible new job she was about to start, but Ray knew the job wouldn't last long. His mother preferred to be at home—her most comfortable place to be with a refreshing drink in her hand.

When most boys his age were learning how to ride a bike or throw a baseball, Ray learned about addiction. He learned about the trouble it brought but how easy it was to explain away.

"I never wanted to be a mom or a wife," his mother often said to him, "and I *have* to drink because of you."

Ray also learned how to hide when his mother drank—and on days when she didn't.

Raymond Boyd was a little boy growing up too fast in the world, and he was so entangled with his mother's feelings that he ignored

8

his own. Most of his time was spent worrying about her happiness, because he believed if she was happy, then somehow, he could be too. He did everything he could to try to make her smile so she'd love him, care for him, be kind to him, and give him what he craved most in life: a tight hug and a whispered word: "Everything's gonna be OK." But those words never came out of her mouth.

He often wished to live somewhere else, like at his grandmother's home, where his worries usually seemed to disappear.

But Ray also learned to keep his wishes to himself and to accept his life the way it was.

CHAPTER 3

I t was an hour after sundown on a sticky summer night. The three-lane California freeway glowed a faint orange from the fluorescent streetlights.

His grandmother's house was now miles away.

The car's air conditioner was loud, but it seemed to be blowing hot air his way. Tiny beads of sweat trickled down the sides of Ray's face. He hadn't said a word since being shoved into the backseat, although he seldom spoke when his mother was in one of her moods. Instead, he nestled alongside the car door and pressed his forehead against the window. He looked out at the road and let the vibrations on the glass massage his brow. His eyes followed the freeway moving underneath him as he focused on the dozens of swaying parallel lines grooved into the concrete. Soon Ray became entranced by the endless waves dancing for him and somehow pushing his worries further and further away.

Thoughts of his grandmother and what she had said about God came to him.

He wants us to return home? he thought. *Why? What's there?*

A few more miles down the road, his mother started shouting the word *fuck* over and over. Ray's shoulders and neck tightened, and he palmed his ears and closed his eyes, just as he did when trouble began at home. But he quickly found he couldn't hide from her this time.

"You're such a fucking idiot!" she screamed.

Ray had often heard people say that his mother was a beautiful woman, and he understood why. She had lush, full lips; sharp cheekbones; a thin nose; and enthralling green eyes, and her hair always flowed gently below her broad shoulders.

But Ray mostly saw her when she was angry—when her eyes turned forest green and narrow and her nostrils flared. She always seemed ready to throw a punch, and he feared he'd be the one to receive it. Nothing seemed scarier to Ray—or uglier—than knowing his mother was upset with him. But that night, on the drive home from his grandmother's house, his mother's sight was focused on his father, and with each passing mile, her voice seemed to get louder, and her words turned meaner.

"What did you say?" she shouted at his father.

Ray slowly opened his eyes to see her lean across the center console. His stomach tightened, while his arms grew weak.

His father didn't answer, seeming to sort through his thoughts, which triggered his mother even more. Ray watched him grip the steering wheel tightly and hold his stare on the road ahead.

"Are you really just going to keep your mouth shut like a fucking idiot?" she asked.

"What do you want from me, Ev?" his father answered.

"I want to know why you told her I got fired!" she shouted.

"I told you. I didn't."

"Well, you must've said something to her."

"All I said was you weren't working anymore. That's it."

"You're so fucking stupid!" she screamed. "I told you not to tell her *anything*, didn't I?"

"Yeah, but she asked. And I didn't know—"

"I didn't know, I didn't know." She quickly interrupted him, mocking him in her schoolgirl's voice. "Why didn't you just say that?" she asked, resuming her raspy tone. "Why didn't you just tell her you didn't know?"

His father held in his answer.

"Well?" She pushed at him.

"I don't know!" his father said, raising his voice now. "I didn't want to lie to her!"

"Why not?" she screamed.

"I'm not like you!" he shouted back at her.

Ray watched his mother pull back her arm as though she were about to take a swing or pull on his hair. He'd seen her do both to him many times before. But she somehow refrained this time, and instead, she pointed and cursed at him more. Ray listened as she told him why she hated him so much and insisted she had lived a better life before they married.

"My life is ruined because of you," she said while jabbing her finger in his father's face. "And because of him!" Holding her glare, she used her thumb to gesture toward Ray.

Ray heard her say things like that often and always tried to avoid the sharp sting that tore behind his eyes, but he never could.

"My mom hates you anyway!" she shouted at his father. "She probably hates you more than I do. She's always hated you!"

Ray knew what she was saying wasn't true, but it didn't stop the pain from surging. He needed to cover his ears. This time, though, he used the cuffs of his long-sleeved shirt as earmuffs. The shirt, his only good one, was navy blue with a button-down collar. His mother had told him earlier that morning, "You had better take good care of it, or I'm going to take care of you!" But Ray decided that getting caught stretching out his sleeves was worth the risk.

He closed his eyes. After several long seconds, everything seemed to fall quiet. His mother's voice had somehow vanished. The only sounds he could hear now were the cars on the road, and the more he focused on them, the more he forgot about everything else.

Ray started playing the guessing game his father had taught him years ago: he'd listen to the passing cars—their engine roars and the growls of the mufflers—and try to figure out what kinds of cars were out there.

The first one he guessed at sounded like a hummingbird, with a high-pitched fluttering sound, only louder. Ray knew what it was immediately. A teenage boy who lived across the street from him drove an old Volkswagen Bug. Ray pictured it in his mind: a bright yellow VW with a reddish-brown passenger door and a big dent on the left front fender. He'd have recognized that car's sound anywhere. To make sure, though, he glanced out the window, and he saw a powder-blue VW Bug putter by, with two little tailpipes sticking out the back.

He returned to closing his eyes.

The next sound was a low, loud gurgling, and it stormed right by his window at high speed. He heard the zooming sound again and again. After the second one, he easily knew what they were. He lifted his head and counted seven motorcycles moving past their car.

Those are so cool, he thought, which made him smile for just the second time that day.

He closed his eyes once again.

He next heard a loud rumbling. It sounded like a big, threatening eighteen-wheel tractor trailer carrying a heavy load. He listened to the motor churning as it moved closer to their car. The sound got louder, and it was somehow staying right outside his window.

Huh?

Ray opened his eyes to get a look, but a heavy white fog had mysteriously entered their car and surrounded him. He could see only a thick cloud that seemed to be touching and breathing on him. He quickly remembered the fog from a time long before, but he couldn't pinpoint when. The one thing he knew for sure was that he wanted it to go away. Something about it terrified him.

He scrunched his eyes and pressed his ears even harder. *Please go away. Please go away,* he wished.

Suddenly, the thundering sounds of the semi turned into the

stuttering noises of an old flatbed truck with narrow wooden spoke wheels that looked as if they belonged on a bicycle and a clunky motor that pushed the speed limit at thirty miles per hour. The sound was unmistakable: *Putt! Putt! Putt!*

Ray somehow knew a lot about the truck, because right then, he was sitting in the back of it.

At that instant, Ray's back was pressed against the cab of an old truck, and swirling, dusty winds were blowing around him.

It was early morning. The sun was just inches above the flat horizon.

He sat scrunched between two teenage boys, his best friends he'd known since grade school.

But how do I know who they are? he immediately asked himself.

Cal, his best friend, was sitting to his left, and Boden, his second-best friend, was on his right. The three of them bumped into each other as the truck bounced along a narrow, empty dirt road. Sometimes they bumped into each other for no reason at all.

"This is the best!" Cal shouted as he playfully elbowed Ray in the ribs.

Ray, without hesitating, elbowed him back and smiled. *What's happening to me?* he wondered.

Ray looked down at his clothes and saw he had on faded overalls with a big rip in the right knee, and on his feet were weathered leather boots he knew were his most comfortable pair.

He looked around more and noticed he was holding a fishing pole with his left hand and was gripping the rim of an old metal bucket with the other. He looked inside the bucket and saw night crawlers squirming in a tin can and fishing hooks and weights scattered at the bottom. There was a closed paper bag that he knew contained a thick ham sandwich wrapped in waxed paper, a red apple, and a stack of saltine crackers.

He turned to see his grinning teenage buddies holding on to fishing gear and supplies of their own.

Somehow, Ray knew they were headed to a creek, and it was just another five minutes or so down the road. They had planned to spend their whole Saturday fishing at his favorite spot. Ray knew that because he remembered talking with Cal and Boden about it at school yesterday.

How the—

Just then, a large familiar elm tree appeared off to his right. Ray quickly turned and rapped on the truck's back window. "Here's good!" he shouted to the driver.

The truck slowed, and the driver shifted the gears down until he brought it bucking to a stop. The boys fought through the dust while sliding their butts down the bed toward the rear of the truck.

"Thanks a lot, Mr. Johnson!" Cal shouted out in his squeaky voice.

"Yeah, thanks, Mr. Johnson!" Boden boomed afterward.

Boden was the oldest of them by almost two years and sounded almost like a man.

But how do I know all this? Ray asked himself.

"You got it, boys!" the driver shouted to them while sticking his head out his side window. "Just don't catch them all, will ya?"

"Yes, Mr. Johnson," Cal and Boden said, and they hurried off toward the creek.

Ray rushed over to the driver's-side door. "We'll be making our way back home a couple of hours before sunset, Mr. Johnson," he said over the motor's idling. "And we'd sure appreciate a ride back. Can you keep an eye out for us?"

"Sure thing," the driver said. "I should be headed back home at that time muhself."

"Thanks a lot, Mr. Johnson."

"You got it." The driver returned to pumping his clutch and gripping the shifter.

Ray turned to see that his best friends had already made it to the trail and were waving for him to hurry up and join them.

"C'mon! Let's go!" Cal shouted out to Ray.

"Yeah, c'mon! Let's go!" repeated Boden.

Ray watched the two of them move swiftly through the tall grass. He noticed they were heading downstream instead of going up. "You're going the wrong way!" he shouted, chasing after them.

Yet Raymond Boyd, the little boy, was still sitting alone in the backseat of his family car. His eyes remained closed, and his hands cupped his ears with the cuffs of his best shirt.

"You're going the wrong way!" Ray shouted to his friends again. "Wait!"

Cal and Boden were darting past trees and zigzagging through the trails. Ray heard them laughing at him, teasing him to catch up. But they were going too fast, and they had too big of a head start, because a moment later, they were gone.

Right after that, without warning, Ray's vision vanished. Everything just disappeared.

It was now pitch black and silent.

"Ray! C'mon! Get out of the damn car!" a woman's voice yelled from far off in the distance.

He slowly opened his eyes.

"Wake up!" she shouted.

"Wh-Where am I?" he asked just before recognizing fast-food wrappers and empty cups and cans lying on the seat next to him.

"We're home. Where else would we be? What's the matter with you?" his mother said.

Ray looked outside and saw a familiar white garage door attached to a faded pink house. He realized where he was—and that his fishing trip was over. He spotted his father warily looking back at him from the other side of the car.

"What h-happened?" Ray asked, rubbing his eyes.

His mother reached down to grab his arm. "Get out of the car! And stop rubbing your eyes! How many times have I told you not to do that? C'mon. Get out."

"Evelyn, I can carry him," his father said as he moved toward them.

"No! Leave him! He's too old now. I got him."

What did I do wrong? Ray wondered.

His mother yanked his arm, and he fell to the ground. His knees thudded when they hit the cement driveway. Ray flinched in pain but held in his tears. He knew better than to cry.

"Jesus Christ, Evelyn!" his father shouted.

"Oh, he's not bleeding," she said. "Ray, c'mon. Get up."

Slowly, Ray lifted himself off the ground, brushed off his legs, and hurried his steps toward his home.

"Put your pajamas on, and get in bed. It's late," his mother said, and she turned off the lights in his room and closed his door.

Through the darkness, Ray struggled to find his bottom dresser drawer.

Like most dreamers, Raymond Boyd remembered only the faint whispers of what his mind brought him when he slept. But he knew what had happened in the car that night had been something other than a dream; it had been far too vivid, and he remembered everything about it.

With his covers pulled over his head and with his eyes closed, Ray pictured the deep black color of the old flatbed truck and could hear the clanking of its motor. He saw the burnt-orange dirt trail against the backdrop of thick greenery and heard the shouts of his best friends calling for him.

He thought about it all until his mind grew tired.

It was well past midnight when he eventually fell asleep.

When morning arrived, Ray still remembered everything about his vision, and he wanted to tell someone what he had seen. But he knew he should probably keep it to himself. There was only one person he'd have told anyway, but she was back at her home and likely still surrounded by all those strangers.

Weeks went by, and Ray could barely see the faces of his two best friends. Yet he still wondered where they were and if he'd ever get to see them again.

Months later, Ray's memory of the fishing trip simply faded away, as if it had never happened.

CHAPTER 4

A year passed.

Ray watched his mother continue to lose control of her drinking while his father spent more and more time at his shop. Some nights, his father somehow knew he should stay away from home altogether.

Ray felt abandoned—as if he mattered not at all. He withdrew from his parents and sought refuge in his bedroom, where he'd play his video games for hours on end.

One morning, on what began as a typical school day, he sat at the kitchen table, eating his cereal, when he heard his mother shout from her bedroom.

"Just give it to me!" she yelled. "And it's really none of your goddamn business what it's for!"

Ray looked at the clock on the stove. It was 8:02 a.m. *Dad's still home?*

"If you actually made some money, this wouldn't be a problem, would it?" his mother said. "When are you going to get a real job?"

Ray heard a muffled voice and guessed it was his father's response.

"I never should've married you!" she said.

Ray dropped his head, closed his eyes, and thought of somewhere safe to be. His grandmother's home was usually the first place he imagined himself being. But before he could get there, he heard his mother again.

"I want out of here!" she screamed.

Ray opened his eyes and stared into the big stainless-steel bowl in front of him. It was the one he'd used for his cereal that morning because all the other bowls were piled high in the kitchen sink.

"I want a divorce!" his mother shouted.

Ray picked up his spoon and poked at the soggy flakes floating in the milk.

"I fuckin' hate it here!" his mother said. A loud shatter immediately followed, as though a picture frame had been thrown against a wall. The crash blasted across the kitchen. Startled, Ray dropped his spoon onto the edge of the metal bowl. A ringing sounded.

Baaaahmmmmm.

He heard nothing else.

Several seconds later, the ringing began to subside, and his mother's voice slowly returned.

"You fucking idiot! I never—"

As she was about to begin her next insult, Ray quickly picked up his spoon and struck the rim of the bowl.

Baaaahmmmmm.

The beautiful-sounding chime moved around him once more, quieting everything again.

Seconds later, though, his mother's voice returned.

"Why don't you—"

Ray struck the bowl.

Baaaahmmmmm.

As the bowl sang to him again, Ray started giggling. *Finally*, he thought, realizing he'd found a way to silence his mother.

He hit the bowl three more times that morning, but on the fourth time, the ringing never came. The kitchen fell silent. As it did, he noticed a white fog creep over his shoulders and begin wrapping around him. Ray remembered the mist immediately—a memory flashed for him of sitting with two teenage boys in the back of a truck bouncing down a dusty road. He took in a deep breath and closed his eyes. Before he could exhale, he found himself in another place and time.

Ray was now sitting at a sturdy wooden table in a familiar kitchen, surrounded by people he recognized, though he was sure he was seeing them for the first time.

He saw a man, a woman, and a young boy, and they were all together for breakfast.

A teapot suddenly whistled behind him, and he turned toward it briefly. As he turned back to the people sitting at the table, he suddenly realized who they were: they were his family.

The freckle-faced young boy sitting to his left was his younger brother, who often annoyed him, yet Ray would have done anything for him. The woman to his right, wearing a red-and-white-striped apron, was his mother. She was someone he loved and relied on and sorely needed in his life. The man directly across from him, with broad shoulders and beefy forearms, was his father. Ray knew he was a stern man but always fair and kind. Ray trusted and respected him more than anyone he'd ever known.

He glanced across the table and saw a plate of thick, crispy bacon. Next to it was a bowl of fried potatoes, and he could smell the onions and garlic drifting in the air. A basket of sourdough toast was within arm's reach, and he could see pads of butter still melting on each slice.

I miss mornings like this, he quickly thought.

Ray's eyes returned to the family, and he noticed they were all smiling at him and seemed to be waiting for his next words.

"So what happened to Boden?" his younger brother asked.

"Yeah, Son. Finish your story," said his father.

Ray cleared his throat, as if pausing to find what to say. "Well, he got into trouble," he said, holding in his laughter. "And he's supposed to write a two-page essay on classroom etiquette."

"Oh, jeez. What did Boden do this time?" his mother asked as she got up to make herself a cup of tea.

"He blew his nose on his shirt," Ray said. He was laughing so hard he barely got out the words. His family joined in, and his younger brother slapped his hand on the table, rattling the plates.

"On his shirt?" his brother asked, grinning from ear to ear.

Meanwhile, Raymond Boyd, the little boy, sat alone inside his messy kitchen with his eyes still closed and his arms hanging by his sides. He seemed unaffected by the loud argument happening not far away.

"Did Boden walk around school the rest of the day like that?" his mother asked. "I mean, my goodness. That would be just awful."

"It's Boden, Mom. He doesn't care," Ray said, chuckling while dishing up a spoonful of potatoes.

"I think I should let his mother know, though," she said. "Don'tcha think?"

"No. It's best if you don't get involved," his father said to her.

Just as he was about to say that Boden had been sent home with a note, his vision quickly vanished. The images of the kitchen, with the family he cherished, just stopped.

"Ray! Wake up!"

He heard a woman shout to him and felt a tight grip on his shoulders. He slowly opened his eyes.

"Ray!" she said again, and with one more thrust of his shoulders, she snapped him back to his home.

He immediately winced in pain from his mother's nails digging into him, and he squirmed in her clutches.

"What the hell's wrong with you?" she demanded while she held him steady and stared into his eyes. "Why are you sleeping *here*?"

"I w-w-wasn't s-s-sleeping," he said. "I w-w-went somewhere."

"What do you mean you went somewhere? You've been here all morning."

"I w-w-went somewhere," he said. "I w-was in a k-k-kitchen, and p-p-people were there."

"What people?"

"A f-f-family."

"What are you talking about?"

It was my family, he wanted to say, but he knew better.

"What family?" she pressed.

Ray suddenly found himself tangled, so he turned from her and rubbed his eyes.

"Stop doing that!" she sharply said as she slapped his hands away from his face.

What did I do wrong? he asked himself while looking at her, his eyes wide.

"Jesus! He's just as stupid as his dad," his mother said as she turned her back to him and walked over to the kitchen sink.

"M-Mom, what h-happened to me?" he asked her.

"How should I know?" she answered over the sound of running water.

Afraid, he asked her the only question that made any sense. "Am I d-d-dying?"

"Dying?" she asked, turning to glare at him. "Of course you're not dying. What's wrong with you?"

"Wh-what happens wh-when you d-d-die?" he asked.

She didn't answer.

"Mom?"

"What? What do you want?"

Tears welled in Ray's eyes as his mother continued to ignore him, seeming more interested in the chore she'd been neglecting for days.

His father entered the kitchen. "What's going on, Ray?" he asked.

"It's nothing, Clay! Just leave him alone!" his mother said, quickly interrupting.

His father hesitated but leaned in closer and whispered to his son, "Is everything OK?"

"Clay! I said to leave him alone!" She wiped off her hands on her pajama bottoms and hurried over to where they were. She left the water running in the sink.

"We can talk later tonight, Ray," his father said hurriedly as his mother closed in.

"Like hell you will," she said. "I don't want you near him!"

Ray locked eyes with his father momentarily before seeing him rush to the counter to find his keys and head out the front door, saying not a word.

Seconds later, Ray heard his father's truck back out of the driveway.

"It's time to catch your bus, Ray," his mother said while she grabbed the big metal bowl from in front of him and dropped it into the sink. A sharp clanking sounded as it landed on the other dishes.

Ray winced.

"Did you hear me?" she asked.

He checked the time on the stove clock. It showed 8:15 a.m. He usually left the house by eight thirty.

"B-But—"

"Now!"

I haven't made my lunch yet, he thought.

CHAPTER 5

Ray arrived at his bus stop earlier than normal and without his lunchbox. Tears continued forming but did not fall.

Who were those people? he wondered. *And why did I see them? What's wrong with me?*

All the while, Ray thought of ways to explain to his mother that what had happened was just a mistake and it wouldn't ever happen again. He wanted to tell her he was sorry.

He wondered if what she often said to him was true—that he had ruined her life.

Maybe I'm not good enough, he thought. *And I don't belong.*

There's nothing wrong with you, the voice inside him quickly said.

But why is this happening to me? Ray asked.

You'll see, the voice answered.

When? the boy asked.

But the voice didn't respond.

Though he never liked hearing from it, Ray wanted to know what it had to say this time. That morning, he needed it to speak.

"When?" he asked aloud, and he waited for an answer. But he didn't hear from it again, not for many years.

After returning home from school that day, Ray quietly slipped through the front door, went straight to his bedroom, and closed his door. He pressed the power button on his video game console.

Within just a few minutes, he was right where he'd hoped to be: mesmerized by the elfin characters floating across his monitor.

Ray played his video games for hours that afternoon as time seemed to hold no meaning. Everything about the vision seemed to have drifted away. And the only problems that existed for him were the game's obstacles, which he skillfully maneuvered around.

Sometime later that night, though, his mother opened his bedroom door and brought him back home.

"Ray! Your dinner's on the table!" she shouted.

He'd forgotten he was hungry.

"Did you hear me?" she asked.

"Yes," he answered while holding his focus on the screen.

"Then go eat before it gets cold!" she snapped, and then she went into her bedroom and closed her door.

Ray ate the sticky spaghetti covered with watery sauce as quickly as possible and returned to his room.

The hours flew by once more.

It was close to midnight when he heard his father come home. Ray waited until he heard the chime on the television and the thud of the recliner chair before he snuck out to see him.

"What are you doing up so late?" his father asked him.

Ray shrugged, hoping his father would remember.

"Is it about this morning?" his father asked as he sat up in his chair and muted the television. "You seemed upset. What's going on, Ray?"

"I d-d-don't know," Ray answered, inching closer and resting his hands on the armrest of his father's recliner. "I th-think something's wr-r-rong with me."

"Nothing's wrong with you, Ray," his father said. "Don't be silly."

"How d-d-do you kn-know?" he asked, almost begging.

"I know," his father said.

"B-But—"

Ray stopped when he saw his father turn quickly and peer down the small hallway. His father's eyes widened. Ray turned to see what he was looking at.

"I thought I told you to leave him alone!" his mother shouted as she glided toward them. "Didn't I?"

Ray crawled into his bed that night having decided he'd always keep his strange visions and his feelings to himself.

CHAPTER 6

S omething happened to Ray after that morning. His visions started coming to him more often, about every other month.

He did everything he could to stop them, but he couldn't. However, he discovered if he ignored them right afterward and pretended they never had happened, they would become a hazy memory, like a forgettable dream. Ray found that playing his video games was the easiest way for him to ignore and forget.

So that was what he did day after day.

By the time he turned fourteen years old, Ray had become an expert at a video game called *Fire When Ready*. It was the most sophisticated sci-fi military game ever made. Human soldiers battled against a race of nine-foot-tall multicolored alien lizards for control of their home planet, Alk. The lizards were known as the Margeeg.

The object of *Fire When Ready* was simple: win as many battles as possible by killing the computer-controlled lizards. Gamers earned points from each kill, and the more points they earned, the higher the level they reached. Each level became increasingly difficult.

Ray was one of tens of millions of gamers worldwide who played the game, yet he had become one of the best. He had reached level nineteen a couple of months ago and had only two more levels to go before achieving the coveted master level. Although only a handful of gamers had ever gotten that far, Ray set a goal to be among the elite.

He preferred to play the game alone on what was called a solo mission, but every so often, he played a duo attack, wherein the game randomly selected a partner for him.

One night, Ray partnered with Deegs2106, a thirty-five-year-old retail salesman from Albuquerque, New Mexico, named Sam. Sam was an average player, six levels below Ray, but Ray could tell he was trying his hardest to keep up. In a few short hours, the two of them eliminated dozens of the digital reptilians. Ray killed most of them, of course, earning him the rankings points he needed. Sam, on the other hand, mainly watched and learned.

"Hold up right there," he told Sam through his headset.

"What do you mean, dude? I can't move," Sam answered. "I'm dead. Remember?"

Sam's character had been lying motionless and dripping with blood while waiting for his life to regenerate. He'd had his head torn off by the blade swipe of an unruly Margeeg. Ray had pushed him into the battle, even though he had known Sam had no chance of winning.

Sam had been counting down the seconds for his return—ten more to go before his character sprang back to life.

"I know. Just stay there, though," he told Sam.

"Why?"

Ray didn't answer. He was too focused on sneaking his way closer to the two enemy soldiers who had just killed Sam.

As he moved within range, Ray killed the distracted lizards. He shot the first one with his laser-sighted crossbow, his favorite weapon because of its silence and accuracy. The second kill, Ray's twentieth that night, came right afterward when he dropped down on the scaly enemy from atop a fifteen-foot rock. He clutched his foot-long knife in both hands and struck the reptile right on the top of its head. The alligator-like skull split in two when he lodged the blade deep inside. Fluorescent-green blood splattered across the screen.

"Oh, nice kills, dude," Sam said just as his character sprang back from the dead.

"Thanks," Ray said.

"You're good. You must play a lot," Sam said.

"All the time."

Sam waited awhile before asking his next question. "Is there another way to get to your level?"

"You mean like cheat?" Ray asked.

"No, no, not cheating. I was just wondering if there's an app you use or if you've found a website or something."

"Just play more," Ray said while his eyes remained glued to the screen.

"That's it?"

Gamers always seemed to doubt Ray's abilities, and he usually ignored them. But Sam seemed genuinely interested, so he answered him.

"The more you play, the better you get," he said.

"How?"

"You learn things," Ray said.

"Like what?"

Ray shared what he'd discovered about the game over the years, things like tactics and technical understandings of the weapons. But *Fire When Ready* was more than just a game to Ray. Sure, he had fun navigating around the alien planet and hunting the giant lizards, but it was also his escape. He could leave his home for hours and travel across the universe to the faraway world where all his problems seemed light-years away. Ray often imagined himself living on Alk as a Margeeg, and he pictured where they went, what they did, and how they thought. He'd go into their minds to figure out ways to kill them.

"So let's head straight for their base," Sam suggested while moving his character toward Ray's. "And we should try to take out their alpha. I mean, it's worth a shot, right?"

"Not yet. I need you to g-go around that hill to the south. I'll meet you on the other side."

"But there's another nesting post over there," Sam said.

"I know, but you'll be OK. Just g-go check it out."

"Dude, c'mon. That's how I just died."

Just do what I say, like you've been doing this whole time, he wanted to tell Sam. Instead, he told him, "It'll b-be different this time."

"Yeah? How?"

"Just trust me."

"Yeah?"

"Yeah."

A moment later, Ray watched Sam's character creep in the direction he wanted him to, which put a wry smirk on the boy's face.

Ray was a top-level player because he studied the game. He knew what the best weapons were and when to use them, and his skill on the game controller surpassed almost everyone. But what really set him apart had nothing to do with those things: Ray knew how to manipulate his partners. He knew when and how to make them go on the attack first or remain on the lookout. He also figured out how to convince them to trade him their best weapon or give him their rare life-regenerating magic elixir. His partners usually willingly did what he said, because Ray made them believe that since he was a rising top-ranked gamer, he knew more than they did.

"Dude, I'm under attack. Are you on your way?" Sam asked, nearly shouting into his microphone.

"Yeah. Almost there," Ray said. "Hold on."

"It doesn't look like it, dude. It looks like you're going around the other side. What are you doing?"

I'm doing what you think I'm doing. Ray preferred not to admit the truth. *I'm using you as bait.*

CHAPTER 7

A female employee hurried down the walkway of the large business campus at Orion3 Game Laboratories. It was early morning, 6:05 a.m.

The sky was overcast, and the air was still.

Charlotte Henry headed to her office to prepare for a meeting with her new staff. It was just her fourth day on the job, and the usually reserved twenty-seven-year-old technology executive wanted to make a good impression.

Shortly after she sat down at her desk to send out the meeting invite, an email landed in her inbox.

"Meet in my office when you get in," it said. "We have a busy day ahead."

A quiet moment later, Charlotte turned off her computer and made her way downstairs. She sat alone inside the near-empty employee café while fondling a hot cup of tea.

Orion3 Game Laboratories, otherwise known as O3, was the undeniable industry leader of interactive video games, the kind Ray Boyd liked playing. Charlotte, one of the company's newest employees, recently had been hired to manage the player experience—to make the games even better.

Angus Stone was O3's president and chief technology officer. For the last few days, he'd been showing Charlotte around the campus, giving her personally guided tours. She'd thought yesterday's hours-long walk with him would be the last one, at least for a while, but unfortunately, the message she'd just received told her otherwise.

"Oh, good. You're here," Angus said to her as Charlotte lingered just outside his open office door. "I think you're going to like what I'm going to show you today."

Charlotte gave him one of her expressionless looks.

Not long after their greeting, Angus held the door open for Charlotte to the entrance of Building Three, a sixty-thousand-square-foot four-story building.

The whole way there, Charlotte had just one thought running through her restless mind: *Just let me do what you hired me to do, Angus. Please?*

They entered a dimly lit warehouse-sized room with fifty-foot ceilings. Charlotte was immediately surprised by the warm, moving air but quickly connected it to the high-pitched whirring sounds of hundreds—probably thousands—of machines inside. A few more steps inside, she saw endless rows of seven-foot metal racks. They were all filled with rectangular devices that had multicolored lights on them blinking nonstop.

"I want you to stick around me for another week or so!" Angus shouted to Charlotte over the noisy whir. "I'm rethinking my plans for you."

"What do you mean?" she shouted back.

"I want to put you in charge of something else—but just for a while," he said.

She was about to ask him why, but Angus shouted to her again.

"I want you to really get to know our programmers," he said. "I think you can learn something from them."

"How?" she responded, appearing to hold back her frustration. *I don't learn from programmers. They learn from me,* she wanted to say.

"You've played our games recently, haven't you?" Angus asked.

"It's been a few months, but yes," she said.

"In that case, I'll schedule some screen time for you this week," he said as they stopped in front of a rack holding several smaller machines. "Things move fast around here, Charlotte, so you need to know what the games are about right now."

I'm aware of that, Angus, she wanted to say.

"And I think you should spend a few days getting to know these too," he said, nodding toward the half dozen machines.

"What are they?" she asked, noticing they were different from all the others she'd been seeing, sleeker and with a flat black finish.

"These are going to make your job a whole lot easier," he said. "They're our latest upgrade of servers. Ten times faster than anything you've ever worked with before, with quadruple the bandwidth. And as far as our engineers can tell, there are unlimited client connections."

Charlotte's eyes opened wider as she looked the machines up and down.

"These five servers will soon be replacing all the others in here."

"Unlimited?" she asked. "But how?"

"You'll know soon enough," he said as he typed a message on his handheld device.

Charlotte waited for him to finish and watched him push the Send button.

"I only work with the best, which is why you're here."

Her seeming look of skepticism quickly changed to a confident grin.

"So what do you think?" he asked her.

"I think," Charlotte said, "I can't wait to test them." She pondered the possibilities of an unlimited client-server network that was faster than anything she'd ever used.

Then, out of nowhere, she had a flashback to one of her last interviews with Angus, when they had finalized her starting salary. Charlotte remembered accepting the position for far more than she would've settled for. She hadn't known Angus was prepared to give her whatever she wanted.

"C'mon," Angus said. "Let's get back to the lab." He led her down a long corridor that was refreshingly cool and quiet.

"The programmers you want me to spend time with," Charlotte said. "What did you have in mind?"

"Well, you're going to see right away that they're probably not like the ones you're used to working with."

"Why is that?"

"Most of them don't have a programming background or even a college degree. They're all former gamers."

"Gamers?" Charlotte asked, leering over at Angus.

"That's right. I like to hire young gamers."

"Why?"

"I've learned they're the ones who know how to make our games better. Programmers know how to code, sure, but the ones who play are the ones with the imagination, the creativity."

But they don't know how to program, Charlotte thought.

"We find the best gamers out there, and we teach them how to write code," Angus said. "And they learn to do it faster than you'd expect them to."

"But you said *young* gamers?"

"I did. And the younger they are, the better," Angus confidently said. "I look for teenagers, especially ones who have a troubled home life."

"Why?"

"They usually have nothing to lose. No family, no friends, no one they can trust, and nothing at home they're going to miss. And when they come here, we become their family, and this becomes their home. They'll do anything for us."

"Have you always found your programmers this way?"

"*Our* programmers, Charlotte," Angus said, politely correcting her. "But no, not always. I had a hunch a while back. And it's paid off."

Charlotte nodded, trying to imagine how it worked. "So where do you find them?"

"We have people who go online and watch gamers," he said while he led them inside an elevator. Angus pushed the button for the third floor. "It's easy to see the best, the ones who play at a level above the others. And when we find someone, we see if he or she fits the profile."

She nodded again while her mind kept returning to the servers in the data center.

"You'll get to meet our programmers soon enough." Angus paused. "But there's one in particular I want to introduce you to now," he said as they made their way inside O3's control room.

The control room was the most secure area on the campus, located high above the lab floor.

Angus walked over to the panel of mirrored windows overlooking the lab, with Charlotte standing close by. "It's that guy down there," Angus told her, pointing to a young man sitting by himself and working in front of two computer terminals.

Charlotte looked down at him. She noticed the rest of the programmers were at least three seats away from him in all directions. She looked back at Angus with a questioning expression.

"I found him about ten years ago," Angus said. "And he's turned into one of the best programmers we've ever had."

"What is—"

Angus interrupted. "But he's up to something. And I haven't been able to figure out what it is."

"Like what?"

"I'm not sure. It might be nothing, but I want you to look at his work and tell me if you see anything out of the ordinary."

"I can do that."

"Good."

"What's his name?" Charlotte asked with her eyes fixed on him.

"His name is Ganesh."

CHAPTER 8

The yelling and fighting between Ray's mother and father never slowed down, nor did his unwanted visions.

Sometimes he'd eavesdrop on his parents, because they often fought about him.

"Why the hell did you take him there?" he heard his mother shout.

Ray was in his bedroom with his door closed. It was late in the evening.

"So he could see her before it's too late. What's wrong with that?" his father shouted back.

"You didn't even ask me," she slurred. "She's my mother, not yours, for fuck's sake!"

His father let her talk.

"It's just wrong!" Evelyn cried out. "And you probably just made her worse!"

Earlier that afternoon, Clay had closed his shop, changed out of his work clothes, and pulled his son out of school for the day.

"I'm taking you to see your grandma," he had told Ray. "She's not doing very well."

"G-G-Grandma's s-sick?"

"Yes, Ray. She's been in the hospital for a few days. And I think you should see her."

"Is sh-she g-g-going to b-b-be OK?"

"Let's just go see her," his father had answered.

Ray had always understood her passing was inevitable; she'd assured him of that. But he had learned how to avoid many painful truths in his life, and her impermanence was one of them.

"I'm so glad you're here, Raymond. I've missed you," his grandmother had said quietly as he entered her room. She'd seemed to smile more with her eyes than with anything else.

"I m-missed you too," he'd said as he scanned the drab and sterile hospital room, eyeing the heavy beige curtain draped around her bed.

Why does she have to be in here with someone else? he'd wondered.

He'd stepped closer and put his hand on top of hers. Right away, he'd noticed how thin his grandmother had become and sensed how weak she seemed to be.

"There's no need to cry, Raymond," she had said.

He'd wiped at his tears with his fingers before his father handed him a small box of tissues.

"I'll always be with you," she had said, and she'd turned her head toward Clay and smiled.

"I'm s-s-scared, G-Grandma."

"Oh, don't be," she'd said softly.

"Wh-Why?" he'd asked her.

"I'll be returning home soon, just like I always told you I would."

"C-C-Can you t-t-tell me ag-g-gain?" he'd begged of her.

"I'm going back to heaven, Raymond. To be with God."

He'd stood quietly and listened as his grandmother explained she was returning to heaven and was ready to go. "I've lived a long, good life, Raymond," she'd said. "It's time."

Ray had held back his sorrow while he listened to her. *Is heaven even real?* he'd wondered. *Is God real?*

He'd remained by her side, caressing her hand.

"Did you know you were born in this hospital, Raymond?" she had asked.

Ray had shaken his head.

She'd turned to Ray's father. "Do you remember, Clay?"

"I sure do," his father had said.

"And I remember how you glowed, Raymond," his grandmother had said. "You were the most peaceful baby I had ever seen. And you looked as though you had a secret to tell. I had this strange feeling that someday you were going to share it with me." She'd seemed to implore him with her eyes.

As much as Ray had wanted to tell her his secret, his body had frozen from fear and shame. *What do I say? She wouldn't believe me anyway.*

He'd watched his grandmother strain to squeeze his hand, which had hurt his heart even more. He had looked over to his father and seen him wipe away tears moving down his face. Ray had wiped away his own tears.

"Oh, I knew there was something special about you, Raymond," she had said. "I always knew."

Moments later, his grandmother had drifted to sleep, and Ray had quietly let go of her hand. He and his father had silently stepped out of the room.

"What did my mom say?" Ray heard his mother ask his father.

"Nothing, really. She just wanted to talk to Ray," his father answered.

His mother waited a moment before she spewed the ugly words: "He can't even talk."

Right after she said it, Ray saw a brilliant flash of light, followed by a faint image of a side of a cliff. It disappeared as quickly as it had arrived.

"I hate you!" he heard his mother shout out next.

The image returned. For several long seconds, Ray saw the unmistakable markings of a large canyon and a dry riverbed below it, with bushes and small trees dotting the scene. The colors exploded behind his eyes, earthen deep red and light brown, with beige sandstone all around. The sky above was transparent powder blue with big, pillowy cumulus clouds floating overhead. A hawk circled in the distance, and he squinted to focus on it until it glided away. *Now what's happening to me?* he wondered. It wasn't one of his visions, because the images appeared for only a few seconds, and the fog was nowhere to be found. Yet he knew they were somehow related.

He waited for another to return. As he did, his mother continued. "I fuckin' hate it here!" she screamed.

So do I, Ray thought, and he quickly got up from his bed and went out to the backyard.

It was a dark night, and except for the sporadic outbursts that came from inside his house, the evening seemed peaceful.

"My life fucking sucks!" his mother shouted.

One day she's going to stop being so mean to me. She has to, he thought, forcing himself to believe it. *And one day she'll stop drinking—she has to. And I'll stop having my dreams, and everything will be just fine.*

With the hopes and ideas shifting about in his mind, Ray suddenly heard a familiar voice from beyond the backyard fence, no more than twenty steps away. He recognized the deep, slow-moving voice right away.

"Nothing she says is about you, Raymond," the old man said.

Eddie Awani was Ray's backyard neighbor. Ray had known Eddie nearly all his life. Eddie was also his only friend.

"And I do not think she even knows what she is saying," Eddie said. "I would ignore her. That is what I would do if I were you."

Ray walked over to the fence and peeked through the slats. He saw Eddie sitting alone in a lawn chair by a small fire.

"S-S-Sorry for the n-n-noise," Ray said, almost whispering.

"It is not your fault, Raymond."

"Yeah. I kn-know. B-B-But sorry."

"You should not apologize for what she does or what she says," Eddie said.

"I w-wasn't. I was j-j-just—" Ray stopped himself from finishing. "She's m-m-my mom, Eddie. And b-b-besides, I l-l-live here."

"I know. But you will not be living here for much longer."

◆

It was a summer afternoon, and Ray was just four years old, when he first met the old man. Ray was playing with his toy trucks in his backyard, when he heard clanging and scraping sounds from the other side of the fence. He also heard a strange hum that he first thought was someone singing but without using any words. Curious, he crept closer to the broken-down fence and poked his head through an opening in the boards. Ray saw an old man with shoulder-length white hair, and he was digging a hole with a shovel.

Lying next to the hole was something small, black, and furry.

"I kn-know that c-cat," he whispered to himself. Ray immediately recognized it as the one he'd often seen running in his own backyard. But he could tell something was wrong with it—it seemed lifeless. Even more curious now, he snuck through the broken fence and found a hiding spot behind a tree. He soon confirmed his suspicions about the cat.

Oh no, he thought.

Ray watched the old man get down on his knees, lift the cat off the ground, and gently place it in the hole. The old man pulled at the dirt and packed it down with his hands. The old man stopped humming after filling the grave.

"He lived with me for ten years," the old man said aloud. "I think he lived a good life."

"Wh-What was his n-name?" Ray asked while still crouching behind the tree.

"He never told me his name. So I just called him Cat," he said, and then he looked off into the distance. "But I think he liked his name."

"Cats d-don't talk."

"Oh, but they do. I just do not understand what they say."

Ray thought about the old man's answer and decided it made sense. "What's your n-name?" Ray asked the old man, angling his head around the tree to show his face.

"My name is Eddie. And your name is Raymond," Eddie said as he struggled to get to his feet.

"How d-did you kn-know?"

"I always hear your mother calling for you. Just like she is right now."

The little boy quickly turned toward his home.

"Raaay! Raaay!" his mother shouted.

He said goodbye to his new friend and rushed home to meet his mother, who was standing by the back door.

"What were you doing over there?" she asked him.

"N-Nothing."

"Nothing, huh? Well then, there's no reason for you to be over there, is there?"

"I g-g-guess—"

"Good! So don't go there anymore."

"I w-won't."

But a week later, a gray kitten moved into Eddie's house. The new tenant meowed loudly for Ray to come over to play with him and Eddie.

"He has not told me his name," Eddie said to Ray. "But maybe he will tell you."

Ray inched his way to the kitten and petted it softly. The kitten immediately ignored the string of yarn Eddie held above his head and turned his attention to Ray.

"Hi there. Wh-What's your n-name?" Ray tenderly asked,

42

leaning a little closer. The kitten purred with approval and arched his back toward him.

"He s-said his n-name is G-Goose," Ray confidently told Eddie.

"Goose?"

"Yep, th-that's what he s-said."

"Well, thank you, Raymond," Eddie said. "I am glad someone can understand him."

Later that same day, his mother asked Ray where he had been.

"I was j-j-just playing," he said.

"Where?"

Ray hesitated before answering. "Eddie's."

"Didn't I tell you I don't want you going over there?" she asked.

"Yes."

"I'm not going to say it again. You got that?"

"B-B-But why?" Ray asked, sensing a peculiar fear in her voice.

"Because I said so. And what were you doing over there anyway?"

"J-J-Just p-p-playing w-with G-G-Goose."

"Who's Goose?"

"It's Eddie's n-new k-k-kitty."

"Why would he name his cat Goose? That's just stupid."

"He d-d-didn't. The k-k-kitty t-told me his name."

"Ray, don't be ridiculous," his mother said.

"It's t-t-true."

"You see? Now, that's why I don't want you going over there. He's just an idiot, and he's turning you into an idiot too."

"B-B-But—"

"Did you hear me?"

"B-B-But—"

"I mean it, Ray. And I bet he's probably telling you stupid stories too, about spirits and ghosts, isn't he?"

He shrugged.

His mother made him promise he'd never go there again and made him say he was sorry. Ray always did as she told him to.

But his promise was short-lived, and he only said he was sorry because he had to.

Eddie's house soon became the safest place for Ray to go whenever there was trouble happening at home. While he spent time there, Eddie quietly confirmed his suspicion about Ray: he had a gift, an unusually close connection with the spirit world.

Through the years, Eddie did his best to help the boy realize his potential. But Eddie's knowledge of the spirit world was incomplete, and he knew that when Ray came of age, he would need a true spirit guide—someone who could show him the way.

The old man patiently waited for that day.

CHAPTER 9

Ray stood high on his toes and peeked over the old, rickety fence. He saw Eddie sitting by a fire that flowed out of an old metal drum. The scent of smoking almond wood moved through the crisp night air.

"How old are you now?" Eddie asked him.

"F-Fourteen," Ray answered.

"Old enough to drive now, right?" Eddie asked.

"N-Not yet," he said, smiling.

"Come. Come join me for a while," Eddie said.

Ray squeezed his body through the broken boards, made his way to an old plastic milk crate next to Eddie, and sat down.

"Soon you will be old enough to make your own decisions, Raymond," Eddie said. "And you will go anywhere you want—and do anything you want."

Why does he always say things like this? Ray quietly wondered, which made him smile.

Goose pranced his way into the backyard and sidled against Ray's leg. The cat jumped onto his lap and purred.

"OK, G-Goose," Ray said, gently stroking him from the top of his head down to his tail.

"What is he saying to you this time?" Eddie asked.

"He j-j-just wants me to p-p-pet him. He says you've b-b-been ignoring him."

"That is mostly true, I suppose."

Ray eventually settled into his seat and warmed himself by the fire. Although his mother's shouts could still be heard, she now seemed far away.

"If you could do anything," Eddie asked, "what would you do?"

Ray shrugged. "I d-d-don't know."

"What would you like to do when you are older?"

He thought about it for a while and then shrugged again.

"Does it scare you to think about it?"

Ray nodded. "Sort of," he said while bringing Goose a little closer to his chest.

"What are you afraid of?" Eddie asked.

He answered with a quick shrug.

"You can do anything, Raymond. Anything you want. And you can go anywhere. Anywhere at all."

Ray scratched at the top of Goose's head and turned to look up to the night sky. His thoughts drifted from imagining what it would be like to be on his own one day to believing everything would someday get better. He fantasized about the day when his parents would finally see him and be there for him—like they were supposed to.

He also thought about his visions and wondered if those too would go away someday.

"You do not want to leave your home, do you?" Eddie asked.

"Not really," he answered, looking up now at a cluster of stars in the eastern part of the sky.

"I do not believe it will get better for you at home, Raymond," Eddie said. "I think it will soon get worse."

What do you know? he wondered, looking into the old man's eyes. He wanted to ask but became afraid of the possible answers.

An image of his mother then came to him, when she drank and her eyes turned mean. *What can be worse than that?*

It had become quiet between the old man and the boy.

Eddie's probably right, Ray thought as he returned his attention to the stars. *She's not going to change. But it could get better. Couldn't it?*

After years of silence, the voice inside Ray spoke unexpectedly: *No!*

Goose meowed loudly, squirmed out of Ray's arms, and dashed away.

"Are you OK?" Eddie asked.

Panicked, Ray looked around the yard and over toward his home. It had turned calm without his noticing. *They've stopped fighting and made up*, he thought, wanting to believe it.

"I sh-should g-g-go," he said to Eddie.

"So soon?"

"Yeah, s-sorry."

"Good night, Raymond," Eddie said, and then he grabbed a log to throw into the fire.

"G-G'night," he said, rising from his seat.

Ray snuck back into his room, where he immediately started up his game console. While he waited for the systems to load, he thought more about what Eddie had said about his home life getting worse. That seemed like the truth, but he didn't want to believe it.

The voice inside him spoke once more: *You know the truth. You've known it all along.*

Ray did his best to ignore what he heard by taking hold of his game controller and pressing at the buttons. He rushed to take aim at all his uncomfortable thoughts and feelings, shooting them all down—one tall lizard at a time.

CHAPTER 10

A few days later, Ray found himself in a familiar situation: standing in his backyard with the shouts from his mother echoing in the night.

He spied the orange glow through the slats of the fence, and he seemed drawn to it like a moth to a flame.

"Eddie?" he whispered as he moved closer.

"Yes, I am here," Eddie answered, and he invited him over.

They sat silently for a few moments, uncomfortably listening and waiting for the yelling to break.

"Have you ever talked to her?" Eddie eventually asked.

"Ab-b-bout what?"

"How you feel?"

"No," he said.

"Have you ever talked to your father?"

"No."

Ray's mind quickly drifted to an imaginary conversation with his mother. *There's no way*, he thought, mocking the idea.

"Does she still hit your father, Raymond?" Eddie flatly asked.

Ray wanted to ask him how he knew but decided it had probably been obvious. Instead, he found himself nodding in shame.

"Does she still hit you too?" Eddie asked carefully.

Ray took in a slow, deep breath. "Only when she d-d-drinks," he said, curiously rubbing a spot on his head, just above his left ear. He thought back to the time his mother had punched him so hard he fell asleep. Ray found the knot he'd been searching for and pushed down on it, oddly enjoying the stinging sensation.

"When I was a boy," Eddie said, "my father would hit me too. Sometimes it was when he was drunk. And sometimes when he was not. I remember it always felt the same to me."

"What d-d-did you d-do?" Ray asked, noticing a different connection between them.

"I left my home."

"You l-left?"

"Yes."

"Where d-d-did you g-g-go?"

"Many places at first. Until I could live on my own."

"You n-n-never went b-b-back?"

"I could not do that, Raymond."

"Why?"

"Nothing was there for me."

"B-B-But your f-f-family was there."

Eddie waited a long while to respond, as he often did. "When someone we love passes on, it is hard for everyone."

Ray listened carefully, wondering why Eddie had suddenly changed the topic.

"And we struggle through the pain until it does not hurt as much."

Ray gently nodded his understanding as he thought about his grandmother's passing last year and how it still hurt if he allowed himself to think about it.

"That pain we feel—it is the same when we love someone who cannot control how much they drink. But the pain is always there, Raymond. It does not go away, and it just gets worse."

It became quiet again.

"That is why I never went back, Raymond."

Without needing any further explanation, Ray knew what Eddie was trying to tell him. *All of this sucks*, he thought. *It just sucks.*

"I want you to know there is nothing wrong with you," Eddie said to his friend.

"What d-d-do you mean?" he asked, worried Eddie somehow knew about his visions. *He knows everything else.*

"I thought I was wrong for wanting to leave my family," Eddie said. "But I knew I was doing the right thing."

"How old w-w-were you wh-when you l-left?" Ray asked.

"I was fourteen."

Fourteen? I'm fourteen!

Ray returned his attention to the curious twinkling lights above him, the seven stars clustered in the eastern sky. They appeared to be signaling something.

"I know how much it hurts," Eddie said. "I know what you are feeling."

CHAPTER 11

Months passed, and Ray was now fifteen years old.
One afternoon, he was in his bedroom, playing his video
game, when his father walked in.

"Hey, Ray, you got a minute?" his father asked.

"Yeah," he answered, and he pressed the Pause button.
"What's up?"

"I'm leaving," his father said, showing no emotion.

"Wh-Where are you g-g-going?" he asked, even though he
sensed his father was leaving home—forever.

"Um, I'm moving out."

"Oh," Ray muttered. "Where to?"

"I found a place close to the shop. It's small, but it'll do for now."

"Are you c-c-coming b-back?" he asked, although the answer
was obvious.

"I'm not, Ray," his father said. "I can't stay here anymore."

Right then, Ray saw a side to his father that he'd always wanted
to see—a side that seemed confident and hopeful—and it made him
smile inside.

"One day maybe you'll understand," his father said. "But just
know that this isn't your fault. None of it is."

Ray slowly nodded.

"You're going to be OK," his father said.

"Yeah, I know," Ray said. *So are you, Dad.*

"You want to talk about it?"

"No."

"You're sure?"

"Yeah," he said.

"OK, well, I'll be back tomorrow to get the rest of my things. But if you need anything, just call me at the shop, OK?"

Ray turned away from his father briefly to look out his window. Though the blinds were closed, he knew what was just outside. He pictured all the rusted metal parts he and his father had stacked there over the years. He guessed it would probably take them at least a day to load onto his truck and take to the shop. But then Ray wondered if he'd just leave them behind to rust even more.

He then turned back and saw his father far forward in time. He smiled even more.

"Ray?"

"OK," he said.

"I guess I'll talk to you later then," his father said, patting Ray on the shoulder.

Ray pursed his lips as he watched his father leave his room. After a few seconds, though, he got out of his chair and rushed after him. He caught up to his father in the driveway, right as he opened the door to his work truck.

"B-B-Bye, Dad," Ray said, and he wrapped his arms tightly around him, with his father nearly doing the same.

Meanwhile, Evelyn sneered as she watched them from behind the drapes of the living room window.

Soon after Clay left, Evelyn began searching the house for everything belonging to her husband while carrying a large plastic garbage bag. Photos of Clay, clothes he had planned to get later, and everything else she could find that was his went into the bag and out to the curb. Evelyn stacked four bags along the sidewalk that night, and she even managed to drag Clay's recliner chair out there by herself. There it all sat, several days before garbage day.

In less than twenty-four hours, Evelyn Boyd had practically erased her husband from their home. But the one thing she had to keep, the most visible reminder of him, still lived there.

The days passed, and before Ray knew it, another year had gone by.

Ray's father had become a ghostlike presence, and his mother had turned into an even drunker and more intolerable roommate.

Ray continued spending time in his room and cared only about reaching the master level of *Fire When Ready*.

But every so often, he'd make his way through an opening in the backyard fence to the other side, where friends always welcomed him.

One night, after a particularly bad day with his mother, Ray went to go see Eddie and Goose. As he walked across his backyard and got closer to the fence, he heard Eddie talking with someone. He eavesdropped for just a moment before Eddie called for him.

"Come join us, Raymond. I want you to meet my friend," Eddie told Ray, gesturing to a small-statured man sitting across from him. "He is from out of town."

The stranger had a smooth, stubble-free dark face; shoulder-length black hair; and shiny white teeth that he showed Ray with an ear-to-ear smile.

Ray nodded at him shyly.

"Hello," the stranger said in an inviting way. "I'm Billy." He quickly got out of his chair to shake Ray's hand.

"N-N-Nice to m-m-meet you," Ray said, stuttering more than usual.

"Please don't be so nervous," Billy said while holding his smile. "I'm not important."

"I'm n-n-not n-nervous," he said. "I st-st-stutter."

"You know," Billy said as he returned to his chair, "I've always wondered why it's called that. I mean, that word seems really hard for you to say. Am I right?"

Ray grinned a nervous grin before accepting Billy's words. "I g-guess."

"And what about someone with a lisp?" Billy said. "That word is practically teasing those people."

Ray looked over to Eddie, who seemed to be holding back his amusement.

"Can you imagine what you'd sound like if you stuttered and had a lisp?" Billy asked, laughing. Eddie quickly joined in, followed by Ray.

Ray decided he liked Billy.

Billy looked up at the sky. "Tonight is a perfect night to see the stars," he said. "Eddie and I have been enjoying this beautiful view all evening."

Ray looked up to see billions of twinkly lights across a cloudless night sky.

"Have you ever just stared at them and wondered what's out there?" Billy asked him.

"All the t-t-time," Ray answered while his eyes scanned the untold number of flickering lights.

"Those stars are there to remind us of something," Billy said.

"Of what?" Ray asked after finding his favorite stars, the seven clustered in the eastern part of the sky. He always noticed how they seemed to blink at him as if communicating something in code.

Ray was looking at the Pleiades star cluster and focusing on the one that sparkled crystal green. Suddenly, Ray was reminded of what his grandmother had told him years ago about God. "He wants us to return home to him," he remembered her saying, and he wondered if that was what Billy meant.

"Of ret-t-turning?" he asked.

"Yes. Exactly," Billy answered.

Ray looked over to Billy and saw a strange excitement in his eyes.

"It's not every day I meet someone who remembers," Billy said.

"Rem-m-members what?" Ray asked.

"That they've returned."

Ray shook his head. "I d-d-don't rem-member that."

"Are you sure? Because I saw you looking over there," Billy said, pointing to the Pleiades.

"Why? What's th-there?" Ray asked curiously.

"For generations, people from all over have believed that we came from a place somewhere right over there. And that's where we'll return when our time on earth has ended."

"Wh-Why? Why d-d-do we ret-turn?"

"That's just who we are."

"Wh-Who are we?" Ray wondered aloud.

"We are spirits learning to be human."

Spirits learning to be human? Ray thought. He swore he'd heard that before. *But when?*

The fire crackled and hissed while he pondered.

"Raymond?" Eddie said.

"Yeah?"

"I have told Billy about you."

"Like what?" Ray asked.

"I told him what you are going through at home—with your mother," Eddie said.

"Eddie thought you might want my help," Billy said.

"With her d-d-drinking?" he asked.

"Her problem isn't her drinking," Billy said.

"It's n-n-not?"

"No, Ray. It's her thinking," Billy said.

Ray gave Billy a deep stare. *How does he know what she thinks?*

"She has a false belief of who she is," Billy said. "And she can't see herself any other way. So she drinks to ease her sadness and pain. But as you know, it doesn't work."

Ray pictured his mother when she'd had too much and how it often confused him to see her that way. It hadn't occurred to him she did it to take away her sadness. At that moment, he found a bit of compassion for her that hung in his throat.

"What c-c-can you d-do for her?" he asked.

"I'm not here for her," Billy said. "I'm here for you."

"You're here f-f-for me?"

"Yes, Ray. If you want my help, I'm here."

"How? How c-c-can you help?"

"That's a long answer. But mostly, I can help you find your way."

"F-F-Find my way?" Ray asked.

"Sometimes," Billy said, "people get lost. And they forget where they are going. I help them to remember."

"How d-d-do you know wh-where they're g-g-going?"

"I never know where they're going. I only know how to help them get back to the road they were on. We're all going somewhere."

"W-We are?"

"Everyone has a purpose in this life. But we sometimes forget what it is. Do you know yours, Ray?" Billy asked carefully.

Ray slowly shook his head. *I don't even do anything except go to school and play my video games*, he wanted to say.

You have your dreams, the voice reminded him.

Ray shuffled in his seat as he tried to ignore what he heard.

"Don't worry," Billy said. "With a bit of work, you can find it. And that is something I can help you with—if that's what you want."

He can help you understand your dreams too, the voice said.

Troubled, Ray quickly rose from his seat. "I should g-go," he said.

"I'm sorry. Did I say something wrong?" Billy asked.

"No. I'm j-j-just—"

"It's not easy to trust someone you've just met, is it?" Billy asked. Ray nodded.

"No need to worry. I understand," Billy said.

"Bye," Ray said, and he walked away.

Billy and Eddie remained by the fire and spoke when they knew they were alone.

"You can help him?" Eddie asked.

"When he decides that's what he wants," Billy said, nodding. "Yes."

Ray snuck back inside his home, careful not to wake his mother.

What am I doing? he thought as he tiptoed to his room. *Is this my life's purpose?*

The voice quickly answered. *Of course it's not.*

CHAPTER 12

The days lingered for Ray.

One early afternoon, his mother had more than her usual share, and her insults came at Ray hard and fast and without reason. She no longer cared that his bedroom door was closed.

"Raaaay!" she screamed.

What's your problem? he wanted to answer. *Just leave me alone.*

"Raaaay! Get your stupid ass over here!"

I can't live like this anymore, he thought.

"Raaaay!"

What can I do?

"Raaaay!"

Where should I go?

◆

Ray sat at the front doorstep of his friend's house for several hours, waiting for him to arrive. The early evening had just turned to dusk when the door to Eddie's truck closed.

Eddie greeted Ray with an inquiring nod.

"You're r-r-right," he said to Eddie with a crackling sound in his voice and with his eyes pink and teary. "She's n-n-not going to ch-ch-change. And it's j-just g-g-getting worse."

"It will be OK," Eddie said. "Come inside." He gently held the boy's shoulder as they made their way to the kitchen table.

"I think I n-need to g-go," Ray said finally.

"Have you talked to your father?"

"Yeah. But he said his p-place is t-too small for me."

"I see," Eddie said.

"C-Can I stay with you?" Ray asked.

"No. That will just cause more problems for you—and for me."

Just then, Goose walked into the kitchen and rubbed against Ray's leg. Ray knelt to pick him up.

"I think it is time for you to see my friend Billy," Eddie said, and he took his time to explain why.

Ray listened.

"I have seen you slowly forget who you are, Raymond, and I have not seen you happy for a long time. Billy can help you."

"How?"

"He will teach you how to find your way," said Eddie, "so you can one day be on your own."

Be on my own? Ray wondered.

"Is that what you want?" Eddie asked.

Ray thought hard about Eddie's question. As he did, he stroked Goose's back a little more intently. The cat purred at him with approval, and somehow, Ray could hear encouraging words from the cat telling him to go to Billy's and promising that everything would OK.

It's time, he eventually decided.

"When c-c-can I g-go?" Ray asked.

"We can leave tonight. If that is what you want."

Ray nodded several times slowly. *I'm ready*, he thought.

"Raymond?"

"OK," he said. "I w-want to g-go."

Eddie walked over to the phone that hung on the kitchen wall and dialed Billy's number. Ray listened to what he said.

Several minutes later, with the phone's speaker still up against his ear and the microphone tilted away, Eddie turned to Ray and asked, "Do you know where your birth certificate is?"

"I th-think so," he answered. *That's a strange question*, he thought.

Eddie returned his attention to his call with Billy. "We will leave here in a few hours," he said before saying goodbye.

"Make sure you get the birth certificate," Eddie said to Ray. "Billy said you will need it one day to prove that you are alive."

Prove that I'm alive?

CHAPTER 13

Ray snuck back into his house and searched through the kitchen for his birth certificate. He found it in an envelope in one of the kitchen drawers, underneath his school report cards. Curious, he took it out. He'd seen it before, but this time, he saw things he hadn't noticed, including the time at which he'd been born, the name of the doctor who'd delivered him, and the name of the hospital. He wondered if that piece of paper was indeed the only thing that proved he was alive. *What if I lost it?* he thought. The strange feelings that followed made him protective of it, so he put it back in the envelope and held the envelope tightly between his thumb and index finger.

Ray looked around the kitchen. Though he didn't want to admit it right then, he knew it might be the last time he was there. It was dirty, as usual, but he ignored the urge to clean up. The yellow Formica table caught his attention, where he always ate alone. He slid his fingers across it and felt it wobble, as it sometimes did. He knelt to look underneath and saw that the folded paper that usually sat beneath one of the legs had been dislodged. He fixed it, just as his father had taught him, and it made him smile.

He moved toward his bedroom, but just before he went inside, he stopped and turned toward the living room. Something pulled him to look around in there, so he turned on the lights. He saw their sofa and walked closer. A memory came to him of playing on it when he was younger. Ray realized it had been years since he last sat on it. He looked down at the dirty stains from his mother's food and drinks, and he smelled the lingering cigarette smoke. Then he noticed his mother's impression on the center cushion. He quickly turned off the lights.

Ray made his way to his bedroom, where he began gathering everything Eddie had told him to pack.

"You want to bring as little as possible," Eddie had said. "Because you are starting over."

When he finished packing, Ray sat on his bed and looked around his room. He took notice of everything he'd be leaving behind. He soon realized that nothing in there mattered to him—except for one thing.

When will I play again? he wondered while staring at his video game console. It suddenly dawned on him that he might never play again ever.

He pushed the power button.

For his final two hours at home, Ray played the best he had ever played. He went on a solo mission on the planet Alk and fought the Margeeg by himself. He made kill after kill, and his ranking soared. Word quickly spread through the *Fire When Ready* gaming community about the player smashing all the records. Gamers from across the globe logged on just to watch him play.

The chat room buzzed.

"He's one of the best," Tyler49er wrote.

"The dude is crushing it. Holy crap!" RickyFlash said.

"He probably has a cheat app," PolarSouth wrote.

"There's no such thing, you moron," EatThis said.

"Maybe he hacked the system?" PolarSouth replied.

"That's impossible. Their system can't be hacked," Tyler49er said.

"No system is hack-proof," Chino790 said.

"Maybe he's one of the original programmers," PolarSouth said.

"Yeah. I bet that's what he is. Like a former employee," EatThis said.

"No way. He's just a good player. I've played with him," Deegs2106 said.

The comments scrolled on.

By the time he shut off his game console, Ray stood alone atop the *Fire When Ready* leader board. He had become an online legend and finally reached the master level.

But for some reason, Ray didn't feel like celebrating. He also didn't feel as though he had accomplished anything. He sat on his bed and stared at his blank monitor. He felt empty inside but didn't know why. He wondered if it was because he was alone. Or maybe, he thought, it was because he had nothing else to prove.

Left without an answer, he unplugged his machine and stashed it underneath a pile of dirty clothes in his closet.

CHAPTER 14

Ganesh, the young computer programmer at Orion3 Game Laboratories, had just entered his twelfth hour of programming when the morning light touched the campus.

I'll sleep when I'm done, Ganesh had said to himself hours earlier, right after he gulped an energy drink and set the empty bottle alongside all the others. But when the new day arrived, it brought a feeling of comfort to the young programmer, hugging him like a warm blanket.

O3 security watched his every yawn.

"It looks like he's about ready," a security member told Charlotte over the phone.

"Thanks," she said. "I'll be over in a few minutes."

A short while later, security cameras zeroed in on Ganesh powering down his computers. They followed him into the sleep room, where he climbed into one of the company's state-of-the-art sleep pods. Once inside, he dialed in the temperature to a cool 68 degrees, set the background noise to the sounds of the ocean, positioned himself comfortably on the adjustable memory-foam bed, and closed his eyes.

"He won't be in there very long," Angus said to Charlotte while they both stared at the monitor homed in on Ganesh. "I give him less than an hour in there."

Charlotte gave Angus a curious look and then checked the time on her watch.

"He doesn't know how to rest," Angus said.

"How well do you know him?" she asked.

"I brought him here when he was just sixteen years old. So I guess I've known him for most of his life."

"I've noticed that the other programmers don't really like him."

Angus appeared to smile. "Let me just say this: he's one of the most dedicated employees we've ever had."

"How so?"

"Well, for starters, he's supposed to be on vacation right now."

"So what's he doing here?"

"He's ignoring company guidelines and doing what he wants."

"Does he ever leave the campus?"

"Rarely. He thinks he's in a race," Angus said.

"To finish his updates?"

"No. To get my attention."

"It looks like he's winning," Charlotte said while rechecking her watch.

Angus cleared his throat. "So when do you think you'll be going down there?" he asked.

"In a few more minutes."

"And how much time are you going to need again?"

"Ten minutes, if that."

"And you're sure he's not going to know?"

"Not if I do it right," she said.

Angus cleared his throat a second time. "I'm still not sure I like this idea. It goes against everything we've built here."

"All I'm doing is watching him, just like you asked. I'll shut it down in a couple of days if nothing's there."

Angus held his response.

Feeling the need, Charlotte offered him a way out. "We don't have to do it this way, Angus. I just thought this would be the fastest way to find out if he's doing something he shouldn't be. Just like you asked me to."

"I know he's up to something," Angus said. "I just don't know what."

Charlotte held her attention on her boss, awaiting his blessing.

"Go ahead," he finally said to her, and he turned away from the monitor and headed straight for his office down the hall.

She watched him go inside and close his door. She checked her watch one last time.

Charlotte quietly made her way down to the lab floor and slipped into Ganesh's chair. With surgical precision, the tech wiz connected a handheld device to one of Ganesh's personal computers and started tapping at her screen.

"All right," she whispered to herself, "let's see what you're up to."

CHAPTER 15

R ay walked out of his bedroom with his backpack around his shoulders. It held only clothes and a few personal items.

He closed his door and then turned to face his mother's closed bedroom door. Strangely, he wondered if she'd continue to keep it closed after he was gone. He guessed she probably would. He reached out his hand to touch it but stopped himself within inches.

So long, he thought, and he noticed he didn't feel the sadness or worry he had anticipated. Instead, he looked at his mother's door, wanting to open it to tell her goodbye. For a brief, strange moment, he knew that leaving her was supposed to happen, as though it had been planned long ago.

But the feeling left him as he turned to walk away.

◆

Evelyn had another restless night. She stayed awake listening to everything Ray did. She heard his tiptoeing footsteps, followed by the lights turning on and off in the living room. She heard the opening and closing of his bedroom door and then the strange, unfamiliar rustling noises that came from his room.

I'm sure he's just cleaning up his shit, she thought, and she guessed she had nothing to worry about.

But when the kitchen's aluminum screen door quietly creaked

open and closed for the second time, she had a sense that trouble was close by.

◆

"You can put your stuff in the back of the truck," Eddie said as Ray walked into his kitchen. "It should not take us long to get there." Soon they were driving east along a California freeway.

CHAPTER 16

Billy was walking along a busy sidewalk in South Shore, Lake Tahoe. It was a crisp night in the Sierra Nevada, colder than usual for late June, yet Billy was dressed as a summer tourist. He had on brown leather flip-flops, khaki cargo shorts, and a mostly red Hawaiian-print shirt. His hair was in a low ponytail.

He had just walked past the main entrance to one of Stateline's newest casinos and was now headed to the back of it, to a seldom-used overflow parking lot.

Billy needed to be alone for a while, and he knew exactly where to go. Years ago, he'd found a seldom-used maintenance storage area surrounded by three masonry walls and a wooden gate. The gate had a combination lock, and Billy had figured out the code.

He went inside and closed the gate behind him.

He set his backpack on the concrete foundation, knelt, and took out an old black leather shaving kit bag from his pack. He opened the bag and pulled out a small clear plastic bag, a soot-stained ceramic bowl, and a box of matches. Carefully, he opened the plastic bag and sprinkled from it a white powder into the bowl, filling it halfway. He set it on the ground.

Billy struck a match. Slowly, he passed the flickering flame over the bowl, when suddenly, *poof!* The powder burst into a thick cloud of smoke, and a pearly white plume slowly rose out of the bowl. The smoke smelled awful, like a mixture of burned plastic and dirty animal hair. But without hesitation, Billy moved his face into the lingering cloud and took a deep breath.

He held the smoke in his lungs for as long as he could.

Seconds later, Billy let out a slow exhalation, which made him cough. After a moment, when his lungs had settled, he leaned over the bowl again and took in another deep breath. This time, he held in the smoke even longer. He then tilted his head back and slowly blew it toward the night sky. The smoke burned his throat and lungs, and he coughed until tears ran from his eyes.

Billy began traveling into the depths of his mind. He moved softly at quantum speed toward interspace, to a place within the world his body currently occupied. Billy had entered the spirit world, where time collided, where he simultaneously experienced the now and things to come.

The casino was busy and loud. Slot machines ringed and pinged, while players, dealers, and cocktail waitresses shouted to one another. But Billy heard mostly white noise.

He slowly walked by people, lots of them, and frequently had to sidestep them—the ones from the future.

Traveling within the spirit world used to be confusing for Billy, but after decades of pilgrimages there, he had figured out how to tell the difference between being in that world and being in the earthly one.

The casino's roulette tables were situated in the middle of the gaming floor. Billy sensed his way there, moving through the rows of slot machines and the crowds. Eventually, he spotted a table with just a few players and edged his way to an open position next to the wheel.

To the right of Billy stood a heavyset middle-aged couple, and to the right of them were two young women who both looked to be in their early twenties. Next to them were two men who appeared to be in their late thirties. The men had been pursuing the two young women for most of the night.

Billy waited for the dealer to finish stacking the casino's winnings from the spin before into towers twenty chips high. Meanwhile, the players hustled to place their bets for the next spin. Arms crisscrossed and elbows bumped as they reached across the green felt.

Billy closed his eyes and looked for the future. Time continued to bend. It was just a matter of moments until he saw what he had come there to see.

He turned his head toward the lit panel near the roulette wheel. Something started blipping. His closed eyes saw a two and a six, and the numbers merged into twenty-six. The number was pixelating as if dancing for him. Billy opened his eyes, and the number twenty-six flashed on the panel.

He reached into his pants pocket, took out a hundred-dollar bill, and set it on the table.

"How would you like this, sir? Dollars?" the dealer asked.

Billy heard the dealer's words warp in an out. "Green, please," he urged himself to say.

"You got it," the dealer said. "Changing out one hundred!" the dealer shouted, and he slid Billy four green twenty-five-dollar chips.

Carefully, Billy reached across the felt and placed one chip on two, one on six, and two on twenty-six. As he did, he heard the mumbling from players around him and saw the dealer try to hide the roll of his eyes.

"That'll be a big win if twenty-six hits," the portly man said to his wife. "But that ain't gonna happen."

"Really? How much?" she asked.

"Let's see," the man said, and he used his index finger to do the calculation on an imaginary chalkboard. "Thirty-five times fifty, five times five is twenty-five, and five times three is fifteen."

Billy resumed closing his eyes.

"Well, I don't know exactly," the husband said, "but it'll be a lot." He then took a swig from his bottle, letting the beer slide down his throat, and ignored the math problem altogether.

Billy heard the dealer drop the white ball and listened to it roll around the spinning roulette wheel. He opened his eyes to see the number twenty-six still flashing on the panel. He closed his eyes again.

Several seconds later, the dealer shouted out, "No more bets!" and then waved his hand across the table.

Even with his eyes closed, Billy saw the ball bouncing up and down. *Clink, clink, clink.* The bouncing eventually stopped, and the ball began spinning around the wheel as though searching for a numbered slot to drop into.

"Twenty-six black!" the dealer shouted, and he carefully set the brass marker on top of Billy's two green chips.

"Shit!" The husband gasped.

"He won," the wife said, although it sounded like a question. "So how much?" she whispered to her husband.

"Hold on," the husband said, raising his beer to his mouth.

The dealer quickly raked in the losing bets and left Billy's two chips alone for all to see.

"How much?" the wife asked again.

"I'm not sure," the husband answered.

One thousand seven hundred fifty dollars, Billy wanted to say to the wife. Instead, he stood quietly with his eyes half closed and his body gently swaying from side to side.

"Paying out seventeen fifty!" the dealer shouted, and Billy saw him look over to the pit boss to ask for permission and receive a consenting nod. "Congratulations," the dealer said, and he slid twelve chips across the felt toward Billy—one yellow one, one pink one, and ten green ones.

"Seventeen hundred and fifty bucks," the husband finally said to his wife.

"Really?" she asked.

Billy looked over to the panel again and saw the next number flash and pixelate.

He placed one green chip on one, one on five, and two on number fifteen. Billy reached for his two green chips still on twenty-six and placed one in his pants pocket. The other he slid to the dealer.

"Thank you, sir. Thank you very much," the dealer said, and he tapped the chip twice along the side of the table.

Meanwhile, the two girlfriends discussed if they should copy Billy's next bet.

"Just bet five bucks," the taller one said.

"Are you sure?" her friend asked.

"Yeah. Just do it."

"Well, I think he's psychic," the wife said to the two young women. "I can see it in him." She put five of her chips on top of Billy's.

"He just got lucky," the husband said. "He's not a psychic."

"Well, I think he is," his wife argued, and she grabbed five more chips, about to increase her bet.

"Don't," her husband whispered as he shook his head. The wife hesitated before putting them back onto her dwindling stack.

"I think he's psychic too," the shorter, prettier girl said before putting her five chips on top of the wife's.

A colorful little tower had grown near the center of the table.

The dealer spun the wheel and released the ball.

After a few seconds, the dealer loudly told the players, "No more bets."

Clink, clink, clink.

The ball stopped where it was supposed to.

"Black fifteen!" the dealer shouted as he placed down the brass marker.

The table erupted.

"How much did we win? How much?" the shorter girlfriend asked.

"A hundred and seventy-five bucks!" the husband answered while avoiding eye contact with his wife.

"It should've been more," the wife said under her breath.

The girlfriends quickly turned to each other and hugged and cheered. The two eager men leaned in closer to them, but the young women politely shooed them away.

"Paying out seventeen fifty," the dealer said again.

All the shouting got the attention of several passersby, and a small crowd gathered around the table. The husband and wife were the first to turn to them, and while they tried their best to explain what had happened, Billy collected his chips and slipped away.

After cashing out, Billy placed one of his newly obtained hundred-dollar bills in his pants pocket, and the rest he put in a hidden pouch inside his backpack.

The next casino awaited him.

By the end of the night, Billy had visited four casinos, while his journey within the spirit world lasted less than an hour.

Upon his return, he showed his gratitude to the Great Spirit as he always did: he found a quiet place underneath the night sky and recited a short prayer to give his thanks to the Great Spirit for keeping him safe and showing him the way.

Afterward, as with all his voyages before, Billy wanted nothing but to close his eyes and fall asleep. Traveling that great distance— through space, time, and dimension—was exhausting for him.

"Where're we going, buddy?" the driver asked after Billy climbed into the cab and closed the door.

"To my home, please," Billy answered, and he handed the driver three crisp hundred-dollar bills.

"Thanks, man," the driver said. He placed the money in his shirt pocket and turned off the meter. "So you win big tonight?"

"Nah, I don't gamble," Billy said while trying to get comfortable in the backseat.

"Yeah, me either." The driver chuckled. "So where am I taking you?"

Billy told the driver his address and then apologized for ignoring him for the remainder of the drive. "I need to rest," he said.

"Yeah, no problem. I'll wake you when we get there. Don't worry," the driver said while turning the taxi onto the main strip of South Shore, Lake Tahoe.

Billy fell asleep right away.

Thirty minutes later, the driver woke him with a question. "Is this where you live?"

CHAPTER 17

"We are here," Eddie said to Ray while carefully steering the truck up a dark and bouncy dirt road.

Ray turned to Eddie briefly before searching through the darkness ahead of them.

During the entire drive there, Ray had been rooted in thought about his decision to leave home. It had seemed unplanned, yet he felt as if he'd been preparing for it all his life. He thought about his mother and how she likely would react after realizing he was gone. *She's not going to care*, he thought, though he hoped otherwise.

Ray also thought about his father and wondered when he'd get to see him again. *I hope he doesn't worry too much.*

For a moment, he considered asking Eddie to turn the truck around because he'd made a mistake.

Mostly, though, Ray was guessing at what would happen during his time with Billy. He'd never been away from home before.

Ray sat up straighter. The enormous forest trees that lined the sides of the road suddenly appeared to him, though they'd been there the whole time. A little farther up, the dirt driveway turned to gravel, and the tires crunched on the rocks and pine needles, sounding like a drumroll.

A lit and expansive ranch-style house then came into view. The dark night surrounded it for what seemed like miles.

Billy lives here? Ray wondered.

Eddie pulled the truck around the circular driveway and parked it by the front door. "We are here," he said to Ray again after turning off the engine.

As they exited the truck, they both noticed the headlights of a car pulling in behind them.

"Good timing, huh?" Billy said to them after closing the door to the taxi.

Eddie gave Billy a nod.

"Everything go OK?" Billy asked.

"So far so good," Eddie answered.

"What's your plan?" Billy asked. "Are you going back now?"

"I think so. They will probably be at my house first thing in the morning."

Who will be? Ray wondered.

"You should get going then. It's late," said Billy. "I've got it from here. I'll call you in a couple of days."

Eddie turned to Ray.

"You c-c-can't stay?" Ray asked him.

"No, I would just get in the way," Eddie said. "Billy will take good care of you now."

This is all happening like it was planned long ago, Ray thought.

"Trust me," Eddie said. "Everything will be OK."

Feeling the need, Ray walked over to Eddie and gave his only friend a hug.

CHAPTER 18

E velyn woke up to her alarm at 5:40 a.m. She wanted to get up early so she could make her son breakfast, which would be her way of apologizing to him for what she had done wrong, whatever that might have been.

She couldn't remember what she had done, but that never mattered. What mattered was getting him to forget it ever happened and to move on.

Evelyn poured pancake mix onto a hot cast-iron griddle. While she did, she thought about starting over and really taking care of herself.

She meant it this time.

I can't keep doing this, she told herself as she noticed the slight trembling in her hands that she couldn't stop.

As the batter started to bubble, the kitchen smelled like a home. A hint of vanilla and cinnamon moved through the air—the secret ingredients Evelyn had learned from her mother. As the pancakes turned a golden brown, she stacked them neatly onto a plate and made a promise to herself. It was a promise she'd made many times in her adult life, but this time, she believed it to be different.

I'm going to quit, she decided as she set down the first pancake. *And I'm going to get better, and everything is going to be OK.* She put down the next. *And I'm going to have a better relationship with Ray because he really is a sweet boy. And I'm going to do it this time because I know I can stop. And when that happens, everything will be better.*

But in the back of Evelyn's mind, the one thing driving all her promises was what she feared most in life: *I don't want to be alone.*

With her pancakes and promises stacked high, she sang loudly to her son from the kitchen. "Ray! Breakfast is ready. It's on the table."

It was now 6:20 a.m.

Not hearing a response, she moved toward his bedroom and knocked on his door. "Ray, I made pancakes."

Evelyn waited before knocking again. "Ray, did you hear me? It's getting late. You should probably get up now."

She leaned her head closer to the door.

Please be home, she silently wished to herself.

She knocked a third time.

"Ray?" she said before turning the knob to open his door.

◆

At 6:24 a.m., Ray slowly opened his eyes. He awoke to feel the morning sun sneak its way through the window blinds and onto his face.

Without knowing the time, he decided it was too early to start the first day of the rest of his life, so he closed his eyes, rolled over onto his side, and drifted back to sleep.

Not long after, he sat at the side of the bed and began massaging his temples and rubbing his eyes. After several deep and relieving rotations, he could hear his mother telling him he'd ruin his eyesight if he kept that up. Ray shook his head, smiled, and rubbed his eyes harder and faster.

After getting dressed, he made his way down a long hallway and poked his head into each of the empty rooms he passed by. It was quiet inside the unfamiliar house, and Ray stepped lightly on the stained-oak floor.

"Billy?"

Ray was in Incline Village, Nevada, in one of the most exclusive zip codes in the world. Billy's home rested on fifteen acres, and it bordered the Tahoe National Forest. Billy's property was one of the most sought-after pieces of land in the area. He'd inherited it from his grandfather a decade earlier. At that time, its value had been in the tens of millions of dollars. It had nearly doubled since then.

Billy had often considered selling his home, but the idea of a wealthy software exec or a Wall Street type taking over his grandfather's sacred land didn't sit right with him, so he planned to keep it for as long as possible—or until the right person came around.

Ray searched through every room, but Billy wasn't to be found. He went outside to look for him.

It was cold that morning, more biting than Ray had expected. He stood on the gravel driveway, right where Eddie had parked his truck less than eight hours earlier, and looked out at a small, lush meadow to the east. Just beyond, Ray saw rows of Jeffrey pine trees and noticed their long green needles and thick brown trunks. He caught a whiff of their sap the second he walked out the door, and the smell of vanilla made him wonder why someone was baking so early.

Ray also spotted dozens of white fir trees, the most towering trees of the forest. Just to the north was an old grove of quaking aspen. He watched their bright green leaves quiver from the slight breeze, and he thought he heard them whispering to each other.

Everything seemed beautiful to him, and he wondered how he could be the only one there to see it.

He looked for Billy at the back of the house. There he saw a flourishing garden. Five rows of long wooden planter boxes were filled with fruit and vegetable plants, and all around them were colorful wildflowers.

On the other side of the garden, a stone's throw away, Ray spotted a small building that looked like an office or a workroom.

I wonder if Billy's in there, he thought.

He took a few steps toward it and then noticed the door open. Someone walked out. It was Billy.

Ray immediately hid behind one of the planter boxes, a handy skill he had learned at home. When he realized where he was, he wanted to get back up, but staying hidden seemed better than explaining to Billy why he was hiding in the first place. So he crouched behind the box and watched Billy go around to the back of the building, toward the forest. Ray crawled through the garden to follow him.

Billy stopped near a small pile of wooden pallets and then slowly walked around them.

What's he searching for? Ray wondered.

Billy grabbed a water hose and began spraying the pallets.

Now what's he doing?

Fifteen minutes later, Billy turned off the water and wrapped the hose around the holder. He started making his way back to the house, heading right in Ray's direction.

As fast as he could, Ray crawled back through the garden and sprinted to the house, hoping he hid well.

"Oh, good morning, Ray," Billy said, sounding cheerful, as he walked into the kitchen. "How did you sleep?"

Ray was sitting at a small table, doing his best to hide his heavy breathing. "Good," he managed to say.

"I'm glad you're up," Billy said, and he walked over to the refrigerator. "I was just about to make us breakfast."

But instead of opening the refrigerator door, he turned to Ray and asked, "Is everything OK?"

Not knowing what to say, Ray waited a moment before answering him with a question. "What d-d-do you do here?"

"Oh, lots of things," Billy said as he removed a carton of eggs from the refrigerator and set them on the counter. He then started scrambling the eggs he had cracked into a bowl.

"D-Do you l-l-live here b-b-by yours-s-self?"

"Yes, but I didn't always. This place belonged to my grandfather. And I lived with him until he passed on. And I lived here with my wife for a short time too before she left."

"You're here b-b-by yourself? All th-this is yours?"

"You can say that. But I don't think of it as mine. I'm just taking care of it for now."

"F-For who?" he asked.

"For the people who need it."

"P-P-People n-n-need it?"

"Yes, Ray. People like you."

"Me?"

"You're here because you need my help, right?"

"I g-g-guess."

"So I take care of this place for you," Billy said, smiling.

Ray feigned a smile in return.

"So have you thought about what you're going to be doing here?" Billy asked.

"Yeah. A little," Ray answered.

"What do you think?" asked Billy as he poured the eggs into a hot cast-iron pan, and they sizzled.

"I'm n-n-not sure."

"Well, you're going to be doing a lot of things—things you're probably not used to," Billy said while pushing the eggs with a wooden spoon from one side of the pan to the other.

"L-Like what?" he asked.

"Like learning to trust me, for one. And I know that's not going to be easy for you."

Feeling exposed, Ray looked away.

"But we'll get there," Billy said. "I promise you."

Ray turned back.

"And I'm going to be asking you to do a lot of things around here, and I'm going to expect you to do them all without question. You think you can do that?"

Ray waited but eventually nodded.

"You're going to have to really trust that I know what I'm doing when I ask you to do these things. OK?"

"OK," he said.

"You think you can do that?"

"I th-th-think so."

"So we agree then?" Billy asked while continuing to keep the eggs from burning.

"Yeah," Ray answered. *How many times do I have to say it?* he wondered.

"Good," Billy replied.

"B-B-But what am I g-g-going to do?"

"You're going to learn to trust."

Ray looked Billy up and down and realized he had no other choice.

"Let me show you something," Billy said, and he turned off the flame on the stove. He made his way to a chair at the table. Billy sat up as tall as possible and brought his hands up toward his chest as if showing the size of a fish he had caught. "What do you think the difference between here and there is?" he asked while presenting one hand and then the other.

"What?" Ray asked.

"Please listen carefully. What's the difference between here," he said, looking at his left hand, "and there?" he said, looking at his right hand.

Ray immediately thought it a strange question and just stared at the space between Billy's hands. Within a few seconds, he said the first answer that came to him.

"It's ab-bout a f-f-foot, I g-g-guess?"

"I didn't ask you to guess, Ray, so please don't," Billy said.

Ray heard a slight agitation in Billy's voice that wasn't there, and he sank in his seat, wanting to disappear. "Sorry."

"Don't be sorry, Ray. You've done nothing wrong. But just

answer the question, please. And by the way, your first answer is wrong."

A tightness formed in Ray's throat from the tension he created. He looked back at Billy and slowly recited the question to himself. *What's the difference between here and there?*

"The answer is pretty obvious when you think about it," he told Ray.

I am thinking about it, Ray thought. *But I have no idea what you're asking me!* He looked closer at Billy, who had his arms held out like a robot, and saw his left hand move ever so slightly. *I know what it is*, he quickly said to himself.

"It's a t-trick question," he told Billy.

"It is?"

"Yeah, b-b-because your hands k-k-keep moving."

"That's very clever," Billy said with a grin.

Ray smiled back.

"But that's not it either."

Ray's lips tightened, and in his frustration, he turned and looked away. *This is just a game*, he said to himself. *It's just a game, and he's testing me.*

"I'll give you one more try, Ray. But keep this in mind: everything you need to know to answer this question has already been said to you."

Ray turned to him and asked, "What d-d-do you m-mean?"

"Think back to when you first started school. What's one of the first things you remember learning?"

What is he talking about? he wondered.

"What do you remember learning?" Billy asked again.

"I d-don't know."

"Well, think about it. If you can remember, the answer to my question is easy."

Ray thought about his years in school, from kindergarten and first grade all the way to his first year of high school. *What did I learn first? It must've been to count and to read,* he thought. *But I don't remember doing that.*

"OK, Ray, your time's almost up, and I'm getting hungry," Billy said.

Ray squinted even tighter. *What's the difference between here and there?* he asked himself again before closing his eyes completely. *What's the difference?*

He looked at the space between Billy's hands and then stared at his hands. The answer wasn't coming to him.

"Last chance, Ray. My arms are getting tired."

Ray had nothing to say.

"Time's up," Billy said.

"I d-d-don't know. Wh-What is it?" Ray said dejectedly.

"It's the letter *t*, Ray," Billy said, and he dropped his hands down to his sides.

Ray had a dumbfounded look.

"Do you understand?" Billy asked.

"No."

"How do you spell *here*?" Billy asked.

"H-e-r-e," Ray answered.

Billy waited. Ray held his confused look.

"Spell *there*," Billy said.

"T-h-e-r-e," he said.

"So what's the difference?"

Ray still didn't know the answer.

"One of those words has the letter *t*, and one of them doesn't. That's the difference between *here* and *there*. Do you get it now?"

"I g-g-get it," he said, dropping his head in defeat.

"I'm going to be showing you things that seem very complicated but really aren't. I'm also going to show you things that you think are very simple but really are quite complex. But to see these things, you're going to have to trust me. You think you can do that?"

"Yes."

"Good," Billy said, and he returned to the stove and turned the burner back on.

"When d-d-do we start?" Ray asked.

"What do you mean *when*?"

CHAPTER 19

Detective Carl Anderson wore a dark blue suit and a red silk tie with a white button-down shirt. His blond crew cut stood high and tight, just as it had since he graduated from the police academy seventeen years earlier.

Anderson had a reputation as a good detective, always acting on his instincts, which usually came to him fast.

Soon after knocking on the front door of the Boyd residence, he'd figured out that the case he'd just been assigned—of the missing teen—was just another runaway.

"Is this the first time he's done this?" he asked Evelyn while he sat with her at the kitchen table.

"Yes. He's never been away from home before," Evelyn answered.

This kid left because of her. Case closed, Anderson said to himself. *This place is a mess, and she's still dressed in her damn pajamas, for Christ's sake.*

"Has anything happened recently? Anything that would make him, you know, upset?"

"No," she said.

Anderson watched her movements carefully and gave her enough time to reconsider her answer. He looked over to his partner, Detective Amber Diaz, who stood behind Evelyn. She gave him a slight nod.

"Are you sure about that?" he asked.

"Well, maybe. I mean, his father left about a year ago. It hasn't been easy on him."

"Has he said anything about it?"

"No, but I can just tell he's still mad," she said.

She's been fighting with this kid, and she's going to make me get her to admit it, Anderson thought. *I mean, just look at this place.*

"So he's not with his father right now?" he asked.

"No. I called him already."

"Or maybe with another family member?"

"There's no other family member."

"What about a friend's house?"

"He doesn't have any," she said.

"Your son doesn't have any friends? You're sure about that?"

Evelyn nodded slowly.

"Mrs. Boyd?" Anderson said, prodding.

"Yeah, I'm sure," she said.

"Mrs. Boyd, you reported your son as missing, but do you think he might've just left on his own?" Anderson asked.

"I think this old guy took him somewhere," Evelyn said.

"What guy?" he asked, seeming intrigued.

"There's this old guy who lives behind us, and Ray likes to go over there sometimes. And I know he went over there last night. I heard him."

"Did you check to see if he's there?"

"Of course I did," Evelyn said, nearly growling. "I went there this morning just before I called you guys. I knocked on his door, but no one answered. And his truck wasn't there either."

"What's this gentleman's name?" Anderson asked.

"Eddie something," she said. "I don't know his last name."

"What can you tell us about him?" Anderson asked.

Evelyn was about to answer the detective, when she heard knocking at the front door. She nearly sprinted to it before opening it.

"Have you heard anything?" Clay asked her as he stepped inside his former home.

"No," Evelyn said while stepping aside and looking away.

"You're the boy's father?" Anderson guessed right away.

"Yes, sir. I'm Clay Boyd."

"I'm Detective Anderson, and this is my partner, Detective Diaz."

Clay walked over to them and shook their hands.

"What can you tell us?" Anderson asked him.

"All I know is what she told me," he said, looking over to Evelyn. "She called me this morning."

"When was the last time you saw your son?" Diaz asked, speaking for the first time.

"Probably eight or nine months ago," Clay said.

"It hasn't been that long," Evelyn said. "It was seven months ago. You spent Thanksgiving with him."

Anderson watched Clay give Evelyn a stare and noticed him nibbling on the inside of his cheek.

"Do you have any idea where he might be right now?" Anderson asked, looking at his notepad.

"No," Clay said, "but he called me last week."

"You've been talking to Ray?" Evelyn asked.

"Yeah," Clay said to her, "of course."

"What are you talking about?" she asked. "What's he been saying to you?"

Anderson quickly stepped in. "Did your son mention anything about wanting to leave?"

"Not exactly," Clay answered.

"Does he want to go live with you? Is that what he's been saying?" Evelyn demanded.

"He asked if he could, but I told him I didn't have room for him."

"But you want him with you, don't you?" she said.

"Mrs. Boyd, can we just focus on your son right now, please?" Diaz said to her.

Evelyn sneered. "Just call me Evelyn."

An awkward pause quickly followed.

Anderson asked, "Now, do either of you have any idea where he might be?"

"I already told you. That old guy took him somewhere," Evelyn said.

"Who? Eddie?" Clay asked.

"Yeah," she said.

"Eddie wouldn't do that," Clay said.

"I know he did!"

"Have you gone over to talk to him?" Clay asked, looking at Anderson.

"No, not yet. We'll go over there after we're done here."

"I know him. So if you want me to go with you," Clay said.

"No, if your son's with him, we'll find him," he said.

"He's with him," Evelyn said under her breath for all to hear.

"Is there anything else you can tell us about your son?" Anderson asked them both. "Something that'll maybe help us find him?"

Evelyn ignored Anderson's question and walked over to the couch, where she dropped herself into her usual spot. Detective Diaz followed her.

"Evelyn, what can you tell me about your son?" Diaz asked as she stood close by.

Evelyn sat quietly hugging a pillow.

CHAPTER 20

I t was midday when Eddie heard knocking at his front door.
"Yes? Can I help you?" he asked, smiling at the two police detectives standing on his stoop.

"Hello. I'm Detective Diaz, and this is Detective Anderson," Diaz said.

"Hello," Eddie responded, giving a half smile.

"Do you have a moment, sir?" Diaz asked. "We'd like to talk with you about the boy who lives in the house behind yours, a Raymond Boyd. May we come inside for a minute?"

"I will speak with you here but for just a minute," he said with one hand on the edge of the door and the other pressed against the frame.

"Don't you think it'd be more comfortable if we went inside?" she said. "It's hot out here."

"I am comfortable here."

"I guess this is going to have to do," Diaz said while she looked back at her partner. "Do you know the boy I'm talking about?" she asked Eddie.

"Yes."

Diaz waited for him to say more, but Eddie kept quiet. "And how do you know him?"

"He is my neighbor," said Eddie.

"Is he here?" Diaz pointedly asked.

"No."

She bent her body slightly to peek around Eddie to look inside the house. Eddie grinned at her and opened his door wider to give the detective an unobstructed view. "He is not here," he said.

"When was the last time you saw him?"

"I am not sure. Maybe it was a week ago? It could be less. It could be more."

"He didn't come over here last night?"

"Not that I remember," he said.

"Well, has he ever mentioned that he'd be going somewhere?"

"Not that I remember."

"You're sure about that?" she asked.

"Yes, I think so."

Anderson stepped closer to the door. "Where do you think he is right now?" Redness appeared on the detective's neck, and sweat formed on his brow.

"You are asking me to guess where he is?" the old man asked.

"Yeah, sure. Guess," Anderson said.

"I would guess he is at home."

"Well, he's not," Anderson said. "He hasn't been home all day—and probably all night."

Eddie just looked at the two detectives.

"You don't seem too concerned, mister," Anderson said before looking down at his notepad and flipping through it.

"Mr. Awani," Diaz said, helping out her partner.

"Right. Mr. Awani," Anderson said, returning his eyes to Eddie.

"Should I be?" Eddie asked.

"Well, he's missing, and his parents are worried. They're afraid something may have happened to him."

The old man again kept quiet.

"Are you concerned about the boy or not?" Anderson asked.

"I am not."

"And why is that?"

"Good question," he said. "Because he is not a boy. He is a young man, and he knows how to take care of himself."

CHAPTER 21

Ray's first days away from home were not what he expected. From early in the morning until late at night, he worked hard and by himself. The jobs Billy gave him to do were ones he'd never done before.

On his third day, his task was to clear fallen branches from around the garden and house. Billy showed him how to break them down to manageable sizes to later put through a wood chipper.

"Did you have chores to do at your home?" Billy asked him.

"Sometimes," he answered.

"Tell me what you did."

As Ray shared the things he used to do—washing the dishes, doing his laundry, and cooking his meals—he realized his mother had made him do them at first, but later, he'd accepted the responsibilities as his own.

"You are really fortunate to have learned to do those things at such a young age," Billy said.

"I d-d-don't f-feel f-f-fortunate," Ray said as he strained to break down a long, thick branch with his hands and feet.

"Well, tell me. What do you feel?"

"I d-d-don't know," he answered while clenching his teeth with a closed mouth.

I wouldn't have had to do those things if my mom didn't drink so much, he thought, throwing the broken pieces onto the pile.

"I think it's difficult sometimes to see what we're learning when we're forced to do it," Billy said.

Ray wiped the sweat from his brow.

"And sometimes," Billy said, "when we do learn the lesson, it's usually too late to show our gratitude to the person who made us do it."

"I have to sh-show her g-g-gratitude?" Ray asked.

"Well, sure, if you want to be happy in your life. That's what you want, isn't it?"

"But I d-d-don't understand," he said.

"Have you ever been grateful for her?"

"Not really," he answered right away.

"Tell me, Ray," Billy said. "What is it that you like most about yourself?"

"I d-d-don't know."

"There must be something."

"I'm g-g-good at p-p-playing my v-v-video games," he said. "I like that." *I was the best*, Ray thought to himself, and he turned his back to Billy to smile.

"And why are you so good at it?" Billy asked.

"B-B-Because I p-played a lot."

"And why did you play so much?"

"B-Because I liked it."

"Why?"

"I d-don't know."

"I have a feeling you do. C'mon."

Ray thought about it more. "I g-guess I just w-w-wanted to b-b-be by myself."

"And why is that?" Billy probed even deeper.

"I wanted to be away from my m-mom," he said while reaching down to pick up another branch. He struggled to break the dry limb in half, and as it cracked and splintered, he realized his mother might have been the reason he was such a good gamer. *I guess I probably wouldn't have played as much if it weren't for her,* he reasoned.

Slowly, Ray understood what Billy was trying to show him—that gratitude starts with recognizing when he'd received a gift, no matter who gave it, and regardless if he asked for it.

For the first time in his life, Ray wanted to thank his mother. He held the feeling for as long as he could.

"There's something else you will have to do for her," Billy then said.

"What's that?"

"You're going to have to forgive her."

What?

◆

On the fourth day, Billy showed Ray the proper way to chop wood with an ax. By noon, Ray had cut more than half a cord, which he had stacked along the side of the house, with Billy watching nearby.

"Have you given much thought to what your life's purpose might be?" Billy asked him.

"A little," Ray answered while straining to carry five heavy pieces of firewood to the side of the house. Billy walked with him, empty-handed.

"What do you think it is?"

"I d-don't know."

"Would you like to find out?"

"I g-guess. How?"

"Have you ever heard of a vision quest?" Billy asked.

"No," he answered. "What is it?"

"It's sort of a ritual. Something boys your age will go through when they're ready to step into manhood," Billy said.

"Should I d-do that?" Ray asked, feeling tempted.

"Well," Billy said, "you tell me."

For the rest of the afternoon, Ray learned about the sacred rite of passage: a days-long experience alone without any food or sleep. Billy explained it was a spiritual journey for which travelers had to be prepared in their hearts and minds. He also cautioned Ray, saying Ray would have to reach deep into his soul to ask difficult questions about his life.

"Not many people complete this journey," Billy said.

By the end of the day, Ray knew he'd need more time to prepare for the vision quest. By nightfall, he realized that was the whole reason he was there.

At the beginning of the fifth day, Ray noticed the calluses forming on his hands where, just days before, he'd had water blisters. He rubbed the thick, rough bumps on his palms and started to understand how they'd gotten there. He remembered his father's hands and thought about how hard he must have worked to get them that way. He wondered if his hands would someday look like his father's.

While he winced in pain from the soreness in his back and shoulders and struggled to get out of bed, Ray wondered how much longer he'd be working for Billy around the property. He added up everything he'd done so far and noted that Billy always had more for him to do.

A bitter taste formed in Ray's mouth.

After getting dressed, he made his way toward the kitchen, where he heard Billy working on their breakfast. The smell of garlic sizzling in butter drifted down the hallway.

"Ah, good morning, Ray," Billy said.

"Morning," he responded grumpily.

"Your eggs are in the pan. I'll start the toast for you."

"Wh-What are we d-d-doing today?" he asked.

"We're going to be in the garden today," Billy said. "I want to clear off all the pine needles."

"P-Pine needles?" he asked.

"Yes. They need to be picked up."

Ray immediately pictured himself on his hands and knees, grabbing the needles one at a time. He assumed it to be another worthless yet difficult job Billy had made up. However, Billy hadn't yet explained to him that the needles would soon become dry and waxy, preventing anything underneath them from growing.

"So wh-when will I b-be ready for my v-vision q-quest?" Ray asked.

"Soon, I think," answered Billy.

"B-But all I've b-b-been doing here is c-c-cleaning up."

"And you're doing a good job of it too."

"B-But I'm n-not—"

Billy stopped him. "Ray?"

"Yeah?"

"Please remember what you agreed to when you first arrived here."

"Wh-What was that?"

"You agreed you'd do whatever I asked," Billy said, staring at Ray. "Remember?"

Ray nodded. "Yeah, b-but—"

"Trust, Ray. You're going to have trust. Now, do you want honey or jam with your toast?"

On the morning of the seventh day, Ray wanted to go home. His knees, shoulders, and back hurt worse than they had the days before; he just wanted to take a long nap. *He's not even paying me*, he thought. *So why should I stay here and keep doing this?*

But soon after he decided to quit, thoughts about the vision quest came to him. The quest had been nagging at him ever since Billy told him about it days earlier. *It's the whole reason Eddie brought me here, isn't it? It must be.*

Later that afternoon, while on his hands and knees on the front lawn and bent over pulling out another weed, he decided to talk with Billy about it.

"Hey, B-Billy?"

Billy was sitting on a lawn chair, taking in the sun's warmth. "Yes?"

"When d-d-do you think I'll b-b-be ready f-f-for the v-v-vision quest?" Ray asked while continuing to dig at the weed with a screwdriver. He was careful to keep the root intact, just as Billy had shown him.

"I think we will both know," Billy answered.

With a few short tugs, the root squeezed out of the ground, causing Ray to smile for the first time in a few days. He held it up for Billy to see, but Billy's eyes were closed.

"But I'm curious. Do you think you're ready?" Billy asked.

Ray tossed the weed onto the pile with the others. "I th-think I've always b-b-been ready," he said. He looked over to see Billy now staring back at him with a peculiar look on his face.

"Then I think it is time you told me your secret," Billy said.

"M-M-My secret?"

"You know, the one you've been keeping from me."

CHAPTER 22

"W-What are you t-talking about?" asked Ray.

"I think you know," Billy said. "It's up to you if you want to tell me, but sooner or later, you're going to have to trust someone."

"B-B-But I d-don't have a s-s-secret," he insisted.

Billy got up from his chair. "Years ago, when you were a small boy, Eddie told me about you. He said he saw something in you, and he believed that you had a strong connection with the Great Spirit and that the Great Spirit spoke to you."

"The G-Great Sp-spirit?" Ray asked. "He sp-speaks to me?"

"God," Billy said. "Well, it's *my* God."

"God doesn't sp-speak to me," Ray said.

"Are you sure?"

"Yes."

"I guess Eddie was wrong then. And I guess I was wrong too."

They looked at each other in silence. Seconds later, Billy started making his way toward the house. "Good job with those weeds," he said. "You pulled more than I thought you would." He walked inside, leaving the front door open.

What the— Ray stared at the opening of the door. *You're just going to leave me here?* he wanted to say.

Why would he stay if you're just going to lie him? the voice inside him said.

"But I'm not ly—" Ray stopped when the truth was upon him. He got to his feet and swiped at the dirt on his knees.

"This s-sucks," he said, nearly shouting, and then he kicked the wilting pile of weeds and stomped off toward the meadow. "I want out of h-here."

You sound like your mom, the voice whispered.

"Go away!" he said and started sprinting toward the meadow's edge. All that Ray wanted was to find a quiet place to hide.

But where?

Ray stopped running before reaching the trees, when the truth became too heavy for him to continue on.

Until now, the safest place he'd ever known was in his room back home. But as the idea of leaving Billy's to return there swirled in his mind, he remembered what his life had been like and how awful he used to feel. He knew that living with his mother again was no longer possible.

He turned back to look toward the lawn, the one now free from the weeds he'd just pulled from it. He looked over to the flourishing garden, which, days before, had been covered in pine needles. Ray thought about all the wood he'd chopped and how he had stacked it perfectly on the other side of the house. He looked down at his hands, at his dirty fingernails and calloused palms, and suddenly respected himself like never before. He smiled. He recalled everything else he'd done since being with Billy and became uplifted from his hard work, as if he had grown a few inches taller.

Suddenly, Ray had an overwhelming urge to thank Billy for the things he had taught him. He looked down at his hands again, gently rubbed his calluses, and then used his thumb to massage the achy center of his left palm.

You're supposed to be here, the voice inside him whispered.

Ray took a moment to think about what he'd just heard. *And besides*, he said to himself, *I can't leave now. I'm not finished here.*

He looked out at the deep forest around him. Its beauty grabbed him, as it had since he arrived. For several minutes, Ray just stared at it, neglecting all his thoughts, good or bad.

Soon it became clear to him that he needed to tell Billy his secret. More than that, though, he wanted to tell his new friend how grateful he was for everything he'd learned.

"I'm g-going to tell him," Ray promised to the forest. "I'm g-going to tell him everything."

CHAPTER 23

They spoke little for the rest of the day. Ray was searching for the right words to say, and Billy gave him the space to find them. Halfway through dinner, Ray finally found his courage.

"Hey, B-Billy?"

"Yes?"

"Why are you help-ping m-me?"

"I'm supposed to."

"What d-d-do you m-mean?"

"Well, you're here because you need my help. And I help people."

"Yeah, b-b-but d-do you help everyone?"

"Everyone who makes his or her way here."

"How d-d-did I g-get here?" he wondered aloud.

"The steps of you getting here, Ray, started long ago—before you were even born. And you're here now with me because you need my help."

It's all planned, Ray thought. *I'm supposed to be here.*

Billy had a serious look about him, with his lips pressed tightly and a slow nodding of his head. "Because you're supposed to be here," he said. "And because the Great Spirit wants you here."

"Why?" Ray asked.

"I don't know why. But I know how you can find out."

"How?" Ray asked, nearly begging for an answer.

"It starts by being honest with yourself," Billy said, "and with me."

Ray knew he was stuck, yet he knew how to get out. He gulped in more courage. "Have you ever h-h-had a d-d-dream you were s-s-someone else?" he asked, struggling more than usual with his speech.

"No," Billy answered. "I can't say that I have."

"D-Do you th-think it would b-b-be weird if I d-d-did?"

"No."

Ray knew what he wanted to say next but took his time before he said it. "I have d-d-dreams like that."

Billy listened.

"And I'm a-a-always this s-same b-boy. I th-think he l-lived a l-long time ago."

"Tell me about him."

Ray hesitated before describing the boy, afraid something terrible might happen just by his talking about him. But Billy somehow knew the right questions to ask to ease Ray into it.

"Do you know his name?" Billy asked.

"No."

"What about other people's names?"

Ray closed his eyes and pictured the people from his visions. He told Billy all he remembered.

"Do you know where you are?" Billy asked.

"No," he answered.

"Can you see where you are?"

"Yes, s-s-sometimes."

"Tell me about it."

Ray recalled living on a farm, in a white house, with a big oak tree out front. He saw wide-open space, with wheat fields and cornfields that shifted in the wind.

He saw a small downtown.

"There are b-b-brick b-buildings there," Ray said. "And d-dirt roads too."

"I bet there's a sign on one of those buildings. Try to see it," Billy said.

Ray fought through the hazy memory and pictured the front of one of the buildings he'd gone into. He saw a sign above the door.

"I s-see something. It's a word."

"What does it say?"

It steadily came into focus for Ray. "It says B-Bank," he said, and he quickly opened his eyes.

"Well then, I guess you went to a bank," Billy said, smiling at first. Then he grinned.

"B-Billy, p-p-please t-tell me what it m-means," Ray pleaded.

"It means the Great Spirit is showing you something."

"What? A b-bank?"

"Well, yes. But there's more there for you to see."

"What?"

"This is just the beginning, Raymond," Billy said. "And soon you're going to figure out what it all means. I promise."

"When? Wh-Wh-When will I f-f-figure it out?"

"Soon."

A nagging question came to Ray, one he'd wanted to ask Billy ever since he met him. "D-Do you know what h-happens when we d-die?"

"I believe we return," Billy answered.

"To b-b-be with G-God?" Ray asked, remembering what his grandmother had always said.

"Yes. I think we do for a while. But then we come back here."

"We c-c-come back again?"

"Yes, I think so. I think our souls want to be here. So I think we come back but in a different way."

"How?"

"I think to another life."

Ray studied Billy carefully and heard for the first time in his life words that brought him hope. He grinned inside.

"I have known people who believed they'd lived on earth before. They'd tell me how they'd see themselves living in another place and another time. And they'd tell me these beautiful stories about who they were and the people they were with. And I believed all of them—just like I believe what you're telling me right now."

"Why? Why d-d-do you th-think this h-happens?"

"I think that's just what we do. But I don't know why."

"M-My d-d-dreams are m-memories of when I was here b-b-before?"

"Yes. That's what I think."

"D-D-Do you have them?" he asked.

"Memories of another life?"

"Yes."

"No, I don't. Not many people do."

"Why?"

"Most of us don't have the gift you do."

"I have a g-g-gift?"

"Of course you do, Ray. And it's time you started thinking that way. The Great Spirit is giving you messages—even without you asking or praying for them. That's a gift." Billy waited. "And it also means you very likely have the answer to the one question every person on this earth asks."

"What qu-qu-question is that?" Ray asked.

Billy smiled as he looked at him. "It's the question you just asked me, Raymond, just a few seconds ago."

Ray broke into a puzzled grin.

Billy reminded him: "What happens when we die?"

Ray's grin dropped. *I don't know the answer to that*, he thought. *I've been asking that question my whole life.* Feeling lost, he asked, "C-Can you tell m-m-me more about the G-Great Spirit?"

"That is my God, the Creator of our earth. And that is who I pray to."

"D-D-Does he t-t-talk to you?"

"Well, no. The Great Spirit has never spoken to me directly. Not the way that he speaks to you."

Ray looked out the window, hoping to get a glimpse of God. *Why me?* he wondered. *What's he trying to tell me?*

"The answers will come to you," Billy said. "They may already have."

"What d-do you mean?"

"All the dreams you've had contain the answers. So I think it is time to look closer at them."

"How?" Ray asked.

"First by praying. But also by writing down everything you can remember," Billy said. "Have you prayed before, Ray?"

"N-Not really," he said. But Ray recalled all the times when he had hoped for his parents' fighting to end and for his mother's drinking to stop. He wondered if he'd been praying that whole time.

"Prayers will bring you answers," Billy said, and he sat back in his chair.

Ray sat back in his.

"I want you to repeat after me," said Billy. He then told Ray several lines to a prayer. He said it several times until Ray had it memorized.

"There's more to this prayer, Ray. And over the next few days, I will teach it to you. But for now, say what you've learned three times a day: in the morning, sometime in the afternoon, and before you go to bed."

"I will," he said, showing a big smile.

"Why are you smiling?" Billy asked.

"I f-feel lucky."

"About what?"

"Th-That I'm here."

"Do you think it's luck that brought you here?"

"Yeah, I g-g-guess so."

"What if I told you that you wanted to be here, and you made it happen?"

"Wh-When d-d-did I do that?"

"That's a great question," Billy said. "But I don't know the answer." He laughed. "But what I do know—or what I believe—is that we create our luck because we want it to happen."

"I d-d-don't understand," Ray said.

"You can't pick and choose what you think is luck and what isn't. You either believe everything in your life is one lucky mystery, or none of it is."

"What d-do you believe?" Ray asked.

"I think none of it is luck."

"Wh-What is it th-then?"

"That's something you need to figure out for yourself."

CHAPTER 24

The guest room had a small, lightly stained antique oak desk with a chair that seemed to match. For the first time since arriving there, Ray sat at it, with a pen in hand and a spiral-bound notebook at the ready.

He wrote his prayer on the first page:

> I acknowledge the Great Spirit, the creator of all things. We are in a beautiful dance together, a dance we've always known. From the beginning, we've never been apart and have always been connected. Without me, without you, we cannot be.

He wrote about his visions on the second page.

Ray Boyd Journal

> He lives on a farm. I don't know his name. But his dad is Matthew, his mom is Ann, and his little brother is Richard. He's a lot older than Richard. One summer, he painted the house with his dad. It's white and has a large porch in the front. He has his own room. His two best friends are Cal and Boden. He works on the farm when he's not going to school. He loves fishing and does it whenever he

can. He hitchhikes all the time too, usually to Cal's house or to go fishing or to go into town.

By the time he reached the third page of his journal, Ray started seeing his visions as though they were real memories. Without realizing it, he no longer hid from them and wanted to remember more.

Ray wrote late into the night—eleven pages—when Billy knocked on his open door.

"We have a big day ahead of us," Billy said.

"J-Just a m-minute," Ray said before turning to see Billy standing at the threshold.

"You'll have time to write tomorrow—I promise."

"Yeah, OK."

"Good night, Ray."

"G-Good night," he said as he turned off the light on the desk.

"See you in the morning."

Ray climbed into bed and closed his eyes, and for the first time in his life, he hoped to dream about the boy he always had hidden from.

CHAPTER 25

R ay returned to his journal the following morning before the sun
and Billy were up. But after what seemed like just a few minutes
of writing, he heard Billy call to him from the kitchen.

Breakfast was almost ready.

"Wh-What are we d-d-doing today?" he asked Billy while setting
the table.

"First, we eat. And then you're going to learn more lines to your
prayer."

"OK," Ray said, grimacing. *No working today. All right!*

After clearing off the table, Billy took Ray outside, where they
inspected the kitchen windows.

"I saw you were looking out them yesterday," Billy said. "What
do you think?"

"They're d-d-dirty," Ray said.

"I thought so too," Billy said. "Why don't you go grab the hose,
and I'll get a bucket and some soap?" He went to the garage.

Ray sighed as he stared at the four large kitchen windows.
Afterward, he looked to the front of the house, where he saw the
even larger living room windows. He started guessing at the number
of windows in the bedrooms and bathrooms that he couldn't see.

Later that evening, after dinner, Billy made a fire in the living
room fireplace and invited Ray to join him.

They sat a few feet apart, with Billy on a comfortable dark

leather couch that faced the fire and with Ray in a matching chair just off to the side.

"There was a young woman I worked with," Billy said. "It was many years ago. And she had dreams of living a past life."

Ray adjusted himself in his chair, sitting a little straighter.

"At first, she was afraid of the things she saw, but after a lot of hard work, she realized she had nothing to fear."

"What h-happened to her?" Ray asked, leaning forward.

"She went searching for what she saw."

"What d-d-did she f-f-find?"

"I don't know," Billy said almost apologetically. "I haven't heard from her since she left."

Ray turned away from Billy to face the fire and pondered.

"Maybe she found something, or maybe she's still looking. I don't know," said Billy.

The fire crackled and hissed.

"There was also a boy I worked with," Billy said.

Ray turned to face him again.

"He was about the same age you are now. And he was also afraid of his dreams, but he wanted to know why he was having them. He didn't care about anything else. He just wanted to know why."

"What h-happened to him?"

"I don't know. One day his mother stopped bringing him here. And she never returned my calls. I haven't heard from him or seen him since."

"Oh," Ray mumbled.

"I thought you should know about them," Billy said.

"I underst-stand," Ray said.

They turned from each other. It was quiet between them for a few moments.

"M-M-Maybe," Ray said while staring into the flames, "they j-just didn't like you v-very much." He held a straight face for just one breath before he started laughing.

"Yes, I'm sure that was it," Billy responded, laughing along.

A short while later, Ray excused himself to go write.

"Don't stay up too late. You have a big day tomorrow," Billy said.

"I won't," said Ray while getting up from his chair. "And, Billy?"

"Yes?"

"I'm n-not like them."

"I know."

Several days passed.

Ray had written as much as he could remember of his visions. He had also memorized all the lines of the prayer Billy had taught him.

Ray knew he'd changed but didn't know why or how. He smiled more and laughed often, and that was all that seemed to matter.

"I'd like to see what you've written in your journal, if you're ready to show me!" Billy shouted up to him.

"I c-c-can show you n-n-now!" Ray shouted back.

"No. Let's wait until after you're finished clearing out the rain gutters."

◆

"He always seems to be having fun," Billy said while his eyes moved through the words in Ray's notebook. "And he seems really confident?"

"He is."

"It seems like he's trying to squeeze the most out of life," Billy said.

"He is," Ray said. "L-Like he kn-knows it's ab-bout to end or s-something."

"I like him," Billy said.

"I d-do too," Ray said. *And I wish I were more like him.*

CHAPTER 26

The following morning, Ray and Billy walked together to the far north side of the property, to a place Ray had never been. The trees stood tall, and dry grass and rust-colored pine needles covered the forest ground. Beams of sunlight filtered through the large branches, making the forest bright in some places and shadowy in others.

"I'm not really sure when it fell," Billy said as they stopped beside the remains of a large fallen Jeffrey pine. "But I found it lying here a few years ago, and I've been slowly clearing it away."

A long, thick tree trunk lay before them with roots still attached that looked like a witch's fingers.

Ray studied the once enormous tree carefully, and he wondered why Billy had brought just the three-pound, three-foot-long ax.

"I'm going to give this to you," Billy said, "and I want you to hit this tree and try to split it."

"B-Billy—"

"Let me finish," Billy said as Ray started to object. . "I want you to hit it, but before each swing, I want you to tell me something about your mom."

"What?"

"Here. Take the ax," Billy said, handing it to Ray. "I want you to swing it at the tree. But before you do, tell me something about your mom."

"L-L-Like what?"

"Whatever you want to tell me. It doesn't matter. I just want to know who she is."

"Anything?"

"Yes, anything. As long as you're honest about it."

"OK," he said. *I trust you.*

"And you can stop whenever you want," Billy said.

Ray gripped and balanced the familiar ax, sliding his hands around the smooth wood handle. He took a moment to loosen his upper body by rolling his shoulders and stretching his neck to the sides.

Seconds later, the sharpened, heavy piece of metal floated over Ray's head.

"Well, sh-she's p-p-pretty, I g-g-guess," he said while forcing a smile. He swung the ax at the log.

Whack!

He looked over to see Billy's steady eyes. Ray freed the ax from the log and rested it below his waist. He thought about what to say next. Seconds later, he knew.

"Sh-She d-d-didn't like her m-m-mom," he said, and he brought the ax above his head.

Whack!

He returned the ax to the ground while deciding on his next words. He then slowly brought it back up again.

"Sh-She d-d-didn't like her d-d-dad either."

Whack!

Ray's phony smile quickly disappeared. His lips tightened, and his eyes narrowed. He breathed a bit heavier now, with droplets of sweat growing on his forehead. He chose his next words.

"Sh-She d-d-didn't like my d-dad."

Whack!

Ray paused but just for a moment.

"Sh-She d-d-didn't want to m-m-marry him," he said.

Whack!

He paused.

"Sh-She had to marry him."

Whack!

Ray carefully pulled the ax out of the tree. He took his time to collect himself. He pulled at his shirt, which had sweat marks forming around the collar and armpits. His eyes had turned red, stinging from the saline.

He struggled now to balance the ax above him. His pain was starting to show on his face.

He thought again of what to say next.

"She d-didn't have any friends."

Whack!

He winced at the stinging that ran through his hands and up to his arms. He waited for the pain to go away. He shook his head and lifted the ax high.

"Sh-She likes to d-d-drink."

Whack!

He knew what to say next. He said it quickly.

"Sh-She d-d-drinks too m-much."

Whack!

"Sh-She's a d-drunk."

Whack!

Ray paused. He knew the next words, but he needed all his strength to say them. He gathered his energy, found his courage, and lifted the ax even higher.

"Sh-She n-n-never wanted m-me," he said, and he swung hard.

Whack!

He wanted to go again, but his fingers grew numb, and his arms weakened like jelly. He set the ax on the ground and then stared at the new raspberries growing in his hands. His whole body ached, but he somehow pushed aside the pain. He knew he needed to keep going. He raised the ax above his shoulders and swung at the tree harder.

"She d-didn't want me."

Whack!

He dropped the ax to the ground.

He stared at the scarred and damaged trunk, looking into the deep slices, and then at the scattered wood chips on the ground next to it. Tears rolled down his face, and snot dribbled from his nose, but he paid them no mind. He struggled to catch his breath.

He lifted the ax again and swung at the tree once more, even harder this time.

"She d-d-didn't want me!" he shouted.

Whack!

Drips of blood trickled from his hands. He could barely grip the handle. Yet Ray refused to give up. He lifted the ax again.

"She d-didn't want me!" he screamed.

Whack!

A burst of energy suddenly filled him, and he quickly raised the ax effortlessly, as if for the first time that day. He glared at the tree trunk with a look of rage.

"She d-didn't want me!" he screamed, even louder.

Whack!

His body screamed back at him, begging for him to stop. But he ignored everything except the task at hand. The ax was above his head again.

"She didn't want me!" he cried out for every soul to hear, and he swung at the tree trunk one more time.

Whack!

The ax-head dropped to the ground, and his hands and knees followed. He slowly reached for the handle, but as his fingers wrapped around it, Billy placed his hands upon Ray's.

"Sh-She d-d-didn't want m-me, B-Billy," Ray cried to him.

"I know."

Ray then reached for Billy, but that man no longer knelt beside him. Ray recognized the person next to him and knew it to be the same man who had been guiding and teaching him all these days, helping him to find his way, but Billy seemed different now, because at that moment, Ray's soul had calmed in ways he'd always hoped.

In his eyes, Billy had become a healer, a shaman.

Ray hugged him tightly and cried harder than he remembered ever crying before. "She d-d-didn't want m-me," he said, struggling to get the words out.

"It doesn't matter," the shaman promised him.

CHAPTER 27

Evelyn Boyd entered day thirteen of living alone. It was her sixth day with not a drop of alcohol.

The last few nights had been hell for her, but last night had seemed to be the worst one yet. She had stayed awake the entire night as her body writhed in pain, as though she were tied up and being beaten by a stick. During it all, she somehow had been reminded of everything she'd ever been ashamed of. It was as if someone had been telling her everything she'd ever done wrong, and the only thing Evelyn could do was listen and suffer.

She'd tossed and turned all night in a sticky pool of sweat.

Evelyn crawled out of bed before the sun came up.

She went to her dresser and opened a small wooden jewelry box she kept in the top drawer. There was something inside she needed, something that had belonged to her mother. Evelyn found it and put it around her neck.

She went to the kitchen and made herself a pot of coffee. She sat at the table, on the chair her son had always sat on. Evelyn held her cup with one hand close to her face, and with the other, she rubbed the gold cross that hung from a thin gold chain.

All Evelyn could do was cry.

CHAPTER 28

Detectives Diaz and Anderson sat across from each other inside their often-quiet police station. It had been more than two weeks since they first learned of the disappearance of Raymond Boyd, and they were no closer to finding him than they'd been when first assigned to the case.

"Let's just close it," Detective Anderson said to his partner. "He's run away, and he's gone."

"I really want to know where he is, though," Diaz said.

"He's far away from his mom. That's where he is," he said.

"Yeah, but where? Where do you think he could've gone without any friends or family helping him?" she asked. "I mean, most of his stuff was still sitting in his room."

"It's not our job to find out," Anderson answered.

"Yeah, I know, but—"

"Someone's helping him, though."

"It's that Eddie guy, isn't it?" Diaz asked.

"That's where I'd put my money."

"Yeah, me too."

"Why're you asking? Do you want to pay him another visit?"

"No. He's not going to tell us anything."

Anderson stared at her as if to say, "That's what I've been saying."

They sat for a little while until Diaz finally said what Anderson had been waiting for. "I guess there's not much for us to do," she said.

"So we're just gonna call him a runaway and be done?" he asked, staring at his partner and hoping.

But before Diaz could answer him, her office phone rang. She saw the caller ID and recognized the number immediately.

"Her timing is spooky," she said, reaching for the handset.

"Who?" Anderson asked.

"Detective Diaz," she said while holding her eyes on the dial pad of her phone.

Diaz spoke for under a minute before pushing the speaker button. "You were saying, Evelyn?" Diaz said, and she held a smile for Anderson as she looked at him.

"I was in his room, putting his laundry away," Evelyn said, "and I found his video game machine thing in his closet. I don't know why, so don't ask me, but I plugged it in and turned it on."

"Uh-huh. Then what happened?"

"All these messages started popping up."

"What'd they say?"

"I don't know. I don't know how to open them. I think you should come over and take a look."

Anderson shook his head while mouthing the word *no*.

She returned her eyes to the phone. "OK, Evelyn. We'll be over later this afternoon. Just don't touch anything, and we'll see you in a few hours."

"OK, but hurry. I don't want these messages to go away," Evelyn said.

"Goodbye, Evelyn," Diaz said, and she hung up the phone. She looked over to her partner, who was glaring and holding up a friendly middle finger. "What?" she exclaimed.

They arrived at the Boyd residence late in the afternoon.

"It's in his room," Evelyn said to the detectives, pointing in that direction. "C'mon. I'll show you." She walked them there.

As they moved toward Ray's bedroom, Detective Diaz noticed how clean the house appeared to be. She took a second look at Evelyn and saw the apparent changes in her too. Diaz remembered the last time they had been at the house, when Evelyn had had on her pajamas. But today Evelyn looked showered and put together, dressed in tight jeans and a form-fitting blouse.

Diaz looked back to her partner and saw him trying not to stare at Evelyn's butt.

"It's right over there," Evelyn said, pointing to the flat screen.

Diaz recognized the *Fire When Ready* game loaded on the game console. Ray's soldier character was dressed in military fatigues and holding a crossbow. It danced and hopped in the foreground. It appeared to be prodding for someone to press the Start button.

At the bottom of the screen, scrolling right to left in big letters, were the words, "You have eleven messages."

Diaz reached for the controller.

"You know what you're doing?" Anderson asked.

"My kids have this game. I've played it with them before," she answered, moving the knobs on the red plastic game controller.

Diaz opened the first message, which was from JohnnyMotion5. The three of them read it silently: "Haven't seen you online in a few days. Could use your help to level up. Where you at?"

Diaz checked if Ray had responded, but he hadn't.

The next message was from a different player asking the same question, as was the next one and the one after that.

"Your son must've been good at this," Diaz said to Evelyn.

"He was on it all the time," she said.

Diaz noticed a sense of pride in Evelyn's voice that she hadn't heard before. This aroused the detective's curiosity.

The remaining unopened messages were from other players asking that same question: "Where you at?"

Diaz moved to the last message in the inbox and found a previously read message. "This looks interesting," she said, and she clicked it open.

From: Recruitment Team

Subject: We've Been Watching You!

Dear Ray,

We have been monitoring your play for several months now. You are an excellent gamer!

Would you be interested in learning about our Player Outreach Program? We bring skilled gamers like you to our development center in Seattle, Washington, to improve our games. Most people don't know this, but we learn a lot from gamers like you. Please let us know if you are interested by replying to this message.

We look forward to hearing from you!

Recruitment Team

"Well, well. What do we make of this?" Anderson asked.

"I'm not sure," Diaz said.

"Did your kids ever get anything like this?" he asked her.

"Never," Diaz said.

"When was it sent?" Evelyn asked, interrupting the two detectives.

Good question, Diaz thought. She scrolled through the message to find the sent date. "It looks like he got it just before he left—two days before."

"Did he write back?" Evelyn asked.

Diaz looked over to her and noticed that Evelyn's green eyes had somehow turned a tiny shade lighter.

CHAPTER 29

The lab floor at Orion3 Game Laboratories was bustling. The programmers packed the wide-open room, and their tapping away at their keyboards sounded like rapid-fire shooting. Max, a longtime employee and one of their midlevel programmers, was among them.

He'd been working at the lab for the last five hours, but moments earlier, he had decided the sixth hour was unreachable. He could barely keep his eyes open, and his code writing had turned to gibberish.

With his hands down by his sides, holding a blank stare at his computer screen, he yawned a big yawn as he stretched his upper body.

I'm done, he finally said to himself before powering down his computer.

But just as he was about to get up from his chair, Max saw someone coming briskly toward him. "Oh great," he mumbled under his breath. "How does he always find me?"

Ganesh headed his way.

"Hey," Ganesh said, and he dropped his laptop bag onto the table, crossing it into Max's workspace.

Max gently pushed the bag over to Ganesh's side. "I thought you were on vacation."

"I am."

"So what are you doing here?"

"I'm just cleaning up a few things. It's taken me a lot longer to—" Ganesh stopped himself from finishing.

Max gave him time to continue, but Ganesh chose to fiddle with his workstation instead.

"What's going on?" Max asked.

"Nothing," Ganesh said. "I've just been sidetracked and haven't been able to get much done lately."

"Uh, you're here on your day off. What are you talking about? It looks like you've got plenty of time."

"I'm not talking about work," Ganesh said. "I'm talking about— oh, never mind. It doesn't matter."

"What update are you working on?"

"Fourteen."

"Weren't you just working on thirteen like a month ago?"

"I was."

"How did you get to fourteen so fast?"

"Because I work smarter, not harder," Ganesh said, sounding flippant.

"Don't be an ass."

Ganesh forced a grin and then returned his focus to his computers as they booted up. A moment later, though, Max saw Ganesh casually peer up at the mirrored windows that encircled the lab. Max's eyes curiously followed.

Ganesh whispered, "I want them to know how good I am, Max."

"I'm pretty sure they know," Max whispered back.

"Maybe, but no one ever says anything to me. I mean, I can't remember the last time I got a promotion."

"You know, if you're looking to get moved up to there, that's never going to happen. You know that, right?"

"Yeah, I guess."

"You'd be better off going to work somewhere else."

"I can't leave this place," Ganesh said, looking as if he had plenty more to say.

Max waited.

"I've had offers, though," Ganesh said. "But I just can't see myself working anywhere else. I know I'll just be chasing what we do here. And besides, I'd never get to play our games."

"You've had other job offers?"

"Of course. And good ones too," Ganesh said, "and for way more money."

Max had envy on his face. "So why don't you go?"

"I'm not done here."

"What do you mean?"

"It's hard to explain. I guess I'm just not ready," Ganesh said, typing quickly on his keyboard.

Max watched him work and was still amazed after all these years at Ganesh's unequalled programming skills.

"So are you going to tell me how you moved through release thirteen so quickly?" Max asked. "Did you find someone to help you?"

"I—" Ganesh reached for his headphones and put them on. "I'll tell you later," he said, nearly shouting.

Max gave him a long stare until he gave up. He gathered his things and walked out of the lab without saying goodbye.

As soon as Max was gone, Ganesh put away his work and pulled up another program.

He wrote.

Hours later, Ganesh finished what he'd set out to do.

He pulled up a form on his computer to submit the program to O3 risk management for approval. He loaded it and then just stared at the Submit button.

Minutes went by.

Getting approval from O3 risk management took a long time, usually weeks. They'd put his program through a twenty-six-step checklist, looking for errors, viruses, and any possible company violations. Nothing ever moved forward in the company without O3 risk management's thorough review.

After another few minutes of pondering, Ganesh hit the Cancel button. He decided to wait until tomorrow and to go over it one more time.

However, the young programmer was unaware that Charlotte Henry had already started her review several days earlier.

CHAPTER 30

"What should we do?" Evelyn asked the detectives.

"We can call the company to see if he's there," Anderson said.

"Yeah, that's an idea," Diaz said while she continued going through the message folders. After spending time looking through the folders of deleted, saved, and sent messages, she eventually found what she'd hoped for in the drafts folder.

"What's that?" Anderson asked as he moved closer to Diaz.

"I'm not sure," Diaz said as she opened the message. The address was blank, and the subject was "I'm Leaving."

> Hey,
> I need to leave home to figure something out. I won't be playing for a while. Maybe soon, though.
> See ya,
> DragonSlayer11

"Well, at least we know he ran away," Anderson said.

"Yeah, but where did he go?" Diaz wondered aloud.

"Eddie knows," Evelyn said, nearly shouting. "I know he does."

"And who was he going to send this to?" Diaz wondered aloud.

CHAPTER 31

Ray and the shaman walked back to the house. Neither of them said a word.

The sun shone brightly overhead through the slow, shifting clouds.

"This way," the shaman eventually said as he led Ray to the garden. He stopped in front of a planter box filled with tomato plants displaying nearly ripe tomatoes. "I'd like you to tell me your prayer," he said. "Will you do that for me?"

Ray nodded and gave the shaman a smile. *Of course*, he thought.

With a bit of unease, he cleared his throat. He rolled his shoulders, stretched his neck from side to side, and then cleared his throat once more. Ray closed his eyes and bowed his head slightly.

"I ackn-nowledge the G-G-Great Spirit, the c-c-creator of all th-things," he said. "We are d-d-dancing b-b-beautifully together in a c-c-constant rhythm. Without me and without you, we c-c-cannot be. I am l-learning to hear your w-w-wisdom and to see the b-b-brilliance of what we are t-t-together. We are wr-writing a g-great story, and the answers are unf-folding in f-front of me. I am l-learning to l-listen c-carefully to each m-moment as you t-teach me all the th-things I n-need to know."

As he spoke, tiny energy waves pulsated around his body. A faint magenta color quickly changed to a deep blue and back to magenta. Ray's eyes remained closed as he went deeper into his prayer. His words flowed through him now, and he no longer thought or remembered what to say—he just knew.

His stutter somehow vanished.

"As I become closer to you and more connected to you and all you have created, I become woven into a great story, the story of us all. I am learning to play my part in this story as best as I can. My very existence, my true happiness, depends on it. And during this time, I want to learn to be present and brave, for it is only in these moments that I can know what's true. May I be clear and connected so that I may hear your guidance with the wisdom of a man yet the curiosity of a child. Now is the time."

Ray drew in a breath and tilted his head upward toward the bright blue sky, and with the sun shining down on his face, he continued. "As we move together, each of us shining our light into the darkness of our souls and bringing our songs where silence has lived, may we be comforted with your compassion, Great Spirit, with your healing and your wisdom. May you hold us warmly, guiding us through your beautiful garden and sharing all your creations with us. May this prayer carry my breath, my words, and my actions, and may it bring us closer together forever. I serve you, Great Spirit, now and always."

Ray's eyes remained closed as he held on to his last word.

A moment later, the shaman and Ray became locked in a wonderful stare.

"You changed it," the shaman said.

"I w-wasn't supposed to?"

"You have made it better," the shaman said with a big smile on his face. "You've made it much better."

Ray's face suddenly mirrored his friend's.

"You're ready," the shaman said.

Ray nodded with a grin.

"Tomorrow. First thing in the morning, I'll take you," the shaman said, and then he turned from the garden and walked alone to the house.

Ray smiled with unprecedented joy as his friend stepped away.

CHAPTER 32

It was an hour before dawn the following day.

The shaman walked out the kitchen door alone and headed east. The chill of the damp mountain air caused him to zip his hoodie a little higher.

The stars twinkled overhead.

Having crossed into the national forest, the shaman eventually made his way to an open yet hidden area. A mountain ridge and trees surrounded it like a fort. Wildflowers and grasses blanketed the forest ground. At the center of the opening, resting on a small rising, a circular wooden shed stood alone.

At ten feet in diameter and seven feet in height, covered by a low-pitched roof, the shed was a geometric octagon. The sides had weather-stained wood paneling discolored from years of sunlight, rain, wind, and snow. It looked natural, as if it were a giant mushroom that had grown out of the ground.

With his flashlight at the ready, the shaman carefully walked around the shed while smacking its sides.

It had been about a year since he last saw it, and it appeared sturdy enough to him.

He went through the doorless opening.

His flashlight homed in on the debris scattered throughout the shed. He gathered the small branches and leaves and dropped them onto the fire pit.

Next to the pit sat a large stack of firewood.

After he finished his preparation, the shaman made the long trek back to the house and entered through the kitchen door. Ray was standing by the stove, working on the breakfast he had started minutes earlier.

"Everything seems ready," the shaman said.

Ray gave him a forced grin. "Me too."

The shaman could see the uncertainty in Ray's eyes. "You're ready," he assured him.

"You th-think so?"

"Yes."

"B-B-But what's g-g-going to h-happen?"

"It's different for everyone. But you're going to be OK."

"I'm n-n-nervous."

"How nervous?" the shaman slyly asked.

"I'm s-s-serious," said Ray.

"I know you're serious. And that's why I'm not."

"Why?" he asked.

"Because you're about to meet your soul, Raymond. I'd be worried if you weren't feeling nervous."

They left the house an hour after sunrise.

"Wh-When will you c-c-come b-back?" Ray asked the shaman shortly after they arrived at the shed.

"Soon," the shaman answered, handing him the gallon of water he held. "But try not to think about me. This is about you and your journey. It's about moving forward and leaving everything else behind. And it's about finding your purpose—by connecting with your soul."

The shaman said little else of what was to come. "Remember to say your prayer," he said. "It will help you."

"I understand," Ray said.

"And one more thing."

Ray looked closer.

"You're not alone, Raymond. You are never alone," the shaman said. Then he turned and walked away.

Ray stood outside the shed and watched him glide through the trails and enter an aspen grove, where he eventually disappeared within the assembly of trees. Ray thought he heard a child's faint laughter. He searched in all directions before deciding the wind had played a trick on him.

By late afternoon, Ray had done nothing except sit and think. He recited his prayer several times, but mostly, he just thought about his life and remembered how it used to be. He wondered what it would be like if it changed even more.

Hours went by, and without warning, the day ended, and night arrived. He sat close to the fire and fed it more often than necessary. Throwing in logs and poking at them with a stick helped to keep him from feeling bored. Thoughts of his mother entered his mind. He guessed she was probably in bed at that moment, and he pictured her bedroom door closed halfway.

An image of a Margeeg came to him, followed by another one. He imagined shooting the colorful lizards with his crossbow.

Ray thought about his online friends and wondered if any had risen to the top of the ranks. He guessed at least one of them had. As his thoughts moved about, he found himself frequently thinking of nothing. When that happened, he returned to reciting his prayer.

Early the next morning, just before the sun cleared the mountains, Ray noticed a shadow move across the entrance. At first, he ignored it, believing it was probably a bird or a small animal moving past. But a moment later, he heard a familiar voice.

"Good morning, Raymond," the shaman said while he set down a fresh gallon of water next to the half-empty one. He began pulling logs out of his backpack and stacking them next to the others.

He initially appeared blurry to Ray. But as the shaman knelt to feed the dwindling fire, he steadily came into focus.

Ray watched the shaman draw a circle in the dirt with his index finger. Directly in the center of it, he drew a smaller circle.

Ray held in his curiosity.

The shaman drew four small circles on the larger one—one at the top, one at the bottom, and two along the sides.

"This is your medicine wheel. These four circles out here represent the directions of the earth, like a compass. And they're the spirits of the north, south, east, and west," the shaman said, pointing at the drawing. "This circle in the center is the Creator, the Great Spirit. Please study this."

Ray looked at it and did his best to recall what the shaman had just said.

"Do you have this image in your head?"

There's not much to remember, Ray thought. *It's a bull's-eye and four circles on the outside.* "I g-g-got it," he said.

"Good," the shaman said. Then he stood up and erased everything with his shoe. "After I leave, I want you to make your medicine wheel, except I want you to do it around the shed. And the circle for the Creator goes in here somewhere. Afterward, I want you to place offerings in the circles—those will be for the spirits."

"O-Offerings?" asked Ray.

"Yes. You're messaging the spirits, asking them to join you on your journey. You're offering them gifts."

Ray nodded.

"Are you still following me?" the shaman asked.

"Yes."

"And when you feel you are ready, I want you to call for them to join you. Invite them here, and tell them the gifts you have placed in the medicine wheel are for them. You may need to use your prayer or beg for them to be with you. Just do whatever you can to get them here. Do you understand?"

"Yes, I th-think so."

"Please say it back to me," the shaman said.

Ray repeated the instructions given to him almost exactly, and the shaman seemed satisfied.

"I have a qu-qu-question," Ray said.

"Yes?"

"Where d-do I g-g-get the gifts?"

"Anywhere from around here. The spirits like things from nature or things you've made. But just know that the spirits expect you to put thought into what you're getting them. That's all they care about."

"B-B-But how will I kn-know what's right?" he asked.

"You have to trust yourself."

Ray grew uneasy. "How w-w-will I know?"

"You're going to have to trust yourself," the shaman repeated.

I have to trust myself? he thought again.

"And these offerings matter, Raymond," the shaman warned. "So take your time in deciding what you're giving to each of them."

"Why?"

"Because they may not show up if you don't."

The shed grew even quieter.

"But I'm sure they'll come," said the shaman.

Ray had his doubts. "What d-do I say to them?"

"That depends. What do you want to know?"

"Everything," he said.

"Then ask them everything."

Time suddenly seemed to stand still.

Ray had nothing to say.

"It's time for me to go," the shaman said, breaking the long silence. He got up, and without saying another word, he walked away.

Ray remained by the fire, watching it survive. He wondered if the spirits were real and if they would actually talk to him.

"Maybe Billy's c-c-crazy," he said aloud. "Or m-maybe we b-both are." He laughed.

Ray got to his knees and looked at the spot the shaman had

cleared with his shoe. He noticed he hadn't wiped it away entirely and saw a faint outline of the circles. He retraced them with his finger.

There's a big circle and the bull's-eye and the four small circles around the big one. Easy enough, he said to himself.

◆

The cold, damp forest air surrounded the shed that morning. Ray walked around it slowly, looking for a place to make his wheel. Right away, he spotted a groove in the dirt that went all around the shed. The channel was weathered—by rain, snow, wind, and likely animals—and Ray guessed it was the ruins of someone else's medicine wheel.

He cleared away the growth and debris and retraced the circles with a stick. Afterward, he went inside the shed to search for the center circle, the one for the Creator—the Great Spirit. He spotted it quickly; it had been there the whole time.

His medicine wheel neared completion.

Several trails wove around the shed, and Ray somehow knew the one that veered toward the north was the one he needed to be on.

His steps were deliberate as he searched the ground, looking for something but unsure what.

Right away, two rocks caught Ray's attention. They were both about the size of duck eggs and were reddish orange, with shiny black flakes. The stones were nearly identical in size and shape—they looked like twins. But as he reached down to pick one of them up, he immediately doubted it was a legitimate offering. Something urged him to leave it there. *It takes longer than ten seconds to find a gift for the spirits*, he thought. But just as he was about to toss it back onto the ground, he questioned what he had just said.

Well, how long does it take? I mean, if I find it in ten seconds or a hundred seconds, why should it matter?

He bent down to pick up the other stone, and he held one in each hand. He continued wrestling with the question: *How long does it take to find a gift?*

"What d-d-difference does it m-make?" he said aloud. "What's the d-d-diff—" He started laughing.

What's the difference between here and there? he thought. *What's the difference between ten seconds and a hundred seconds? Between ten and a hundred? I know what it is. It's zero, which is nothing. There is no difference!*

Excitement grew within him, and he quickly put the twin rocks into his pants pocket and went searching for more offerings.

He moved along the trail with a big smile on his face.

As the sun climbed overhead, Ray steadily made his way back to the shed. His pockets were now full of rocks, small pine cones, seedpods, and other found treasures. He also held two feathers and a large piece of snake shedding in his hands.

Once inside the shed, Ray laid all the gifts down on the dirt floor and went through them one by one.

Of the rocks he'd found, he coveted eight of them. He set the remainder off to the side. The two twins he'd discovered right away were his favorites. Ray next preferred a mostly white one with black specks all around it, which was the size of a golf ball. He also favored a shiny, flat black rock the size of his palm and a gray one that looked like an egg but much smaller. Three quartz crystals had caught his attention. He assumed the crystals all had been part of one big crystal before it broke apart.

He also had found two bent finishing nails outside the shed that he thought were interesting, and he wondered if he could straighten them out.

Ray knelt closer to the gifts and started arranging them by size. "Now, who g-gets what?" he asked, hoping his words would somehow bring an answer.

Little did he know, the answers were coming.

CHAPTER 33

Gamblers filled the casino's poker room. The big game, the five-ten no-limit Texas Hold'em game, had been nonstop action for most of the day.

It was now late in the evening in South Lake Tahoe.

"It's on you, Doc," the big man said to the shaman, who sat three seats to his left.

The two of them had been battling each other for hours, and they were now involved in the biggest pot of the night.

It was the shaman's turn, but he hadn't acted for close to a minute. He'd just been staring back and forth between the big man and the scramble of poker chips next to the five overturned cards in the center of the felt-lined table.

The big man had said, "Check," after the dealer laid down the last card. The shaman had been trying to put the pieces of the puzzle together ever since. He'd had the best hand after the flop, a top-end straight, the stone-cold nuts. He held the ten of clubs and the jack of clubs, and when the flop had revealed a seven, eight, and nine, the shaman had had everyone beat. But it had been dangerous for him because the seven and nine were clubs, and he'd known he could lose to a higher flush if another club showed up.

I need to protect my hand, he'd told himself just after the dealer put down the three flop cards. So he'd bet big: $500. The big guy had called, and everyone else had folded. The two of them had then been heads-up.

The dealer had set down the next card, the turn card: the three of clubs.

Shit! the shaman had thought while trying his hardest not to show his frustration.

Without pause, the big guy had checked.

Well, I guess he doesn't have a flush, the shaman had thought. *If he did, he would've bet. He's behind. He must be. He has to be.*

In the poker world, the shaman's hand was a monster. It was practically unbeatable, especially when playing against just one other player. Knowing this, he'd bet $2,000 after the dealer laid down the turn card. The big guy had taken his time, looked at his cards again, and eventually called the shaman's bet.

The pot had neared $5,000.

Why did he call? What can he have? the shaman had wondered.

The last card dealt, the river card, had turned up a blank, the four of diamonds. The big guy had checked again.

If he has a flush, he would've bet, right? There's no full house, so I can't lose. The shaman's wondering was approaching two minutes. *He must have two pair or three of a kind. What else can it be?*

The pile of chips called to him. He had another $2,000 neatly stacked in front of him, and the big guy had well over $6,000 in front of him. Half the big guy's chips had belonged to the shaman earlier in the night.

"It's on you, Doc," the big guy said again while he looked down at his watch.

I should check. He might have a higher flush, the shaman thought. But the gambling addict spoke louder. *I have to be ahead. I am ahead.*

The addict settled the argument.

"I'm all in," the shaman said, pushing the rest of his chips forward.

"Call," the big guy quickly said, and he turned over his two cards: the ace and queen of clubs.

The big guy was the winner.

The shaman was the loser.

The shaman watched as all his chips moved away from in front of him. With the $2,500 he'd lost earlier in the evening, it had turned out to be a typical poker night for him.

An average player at best, the shaman always convinced himself he was good enough to sit at the higher-stakes tables, where the risk and reward were greater. But he always seemed to walk away from the table with his pockets empty.

"Buying in for more?" the big guy asked while stacking his new winnings.

The shaman looked down at his watch. He had planned to be home two hours earlier to check on his student. "No, I should probably get going."

"See you tomorrow?"

"I'll be here," he said.

As the shaman walked away from the poker room, he spotted the roulette tables not far away. He looked at his watch again and then back at the tables and quickened his steps toward the back entrance of the casino.

CHAPTER 34

The sun had long ago been swallowed by the Sierra Nevada mountain range, and the moon was about to be eaten next.

The fire in the shed burned brightly; strange shadows danced around inside.

Ray had been staring at the gifts laid out in front of him, wondering whom to give them to. He set them in the center circle one at a time, but it always seemed wrong.

He went outside with the gifts, and he did the same thing with all the other circles. Still, nothing seemed right.

The hours ticked away like minutes, and morning arrived. Ray no longer had a connection to time or to himself.

"I ackn-n-nowledge the G-G-Great Spirit," he said, struggling to remember the next line to his prayer. "W-We are b-b-beautiful … from b-b-beginning to end, never …"

He paused.

"Without m-me, without …"

He stopped.

The words were no longer within him.

Ray hung his head. "I want to g-go home," he said while his body shifted slowly back and forth and from side to side, aching from hunger and lack of sleep. "I j-just want to l-leave."

He imagined himself standing up and walking out of the shed. He saw his body move quickly along the trails and arrive almost instantly at the shaman's house. But Ray didn't stop there. He continued moving effortlessly down the driveway and to the main road. Soon he was gliding along the highway, on his way home.

He arrived.

Ray watched himself slowly open the front door. Through the cigarette smoke drifting in the air, he saw his mother sitting on the stained and battered couch.

"I knew you'd be back," she said as she raised her glass to her lips and slurped. "I just knew it."

"What am I d-d-doing here?" he said. "I m-m-made a m-mistake. I need to go back." He turned and tried to open the now-locked door.

"Raymond!" his mother shouted. "Where do you think you're going?"

"No!" he screamed, pulling and turning the handle to get the door open.

"Raymond!"

"No!"

Suddenly, he found himself back inside the shed, sitting by the fire. He sighed in relief as a tear trickled down the side of his face.

This is where I'm supposed to be.

It was dark inside the shed now. The mountain had caught its prey once again. Ray could barely see the gifts he had laid out in front of him. He looked at the fire pit to see only a few glowing embers. He grabbed a long stick and poked at them to get it going again. A small plume of smoke rose from the ash, and he watched it disappear. He grabbed a log and threw it in, and as the large piece of wood dropped onto the smoldering ash, a small piece of charcoal landed in front of him. He stared at it and, strangely, heard himself say, "The ball of fire is born in the east, and it dies in the west." Ray had never said those words before or even thought of them. But right then, "The ball of fire is born in the east, and it dies in the west" made perfect sense to him.

"Of c-course. Of c-course that's where it starts," he said aloud.

He reached into the pit and carefully picked up a large piece of charcoal. It was black, light in his hands, and still warm to the touch. He studied it for a long while. He went outside and placed it in the west circle. Afterward, he grabbed several fresh matchsticks and put them in the east circle.

"The b-ball of f-fire is b-born in the east, and it d-dies in the west," he said confidently. After he repeated those words again, the offerings in front of him somehow moved into place.

One by one, Ray knew where everything went. He separated the twin orange rocks to the east and west because they represented the sun's rotation. The white rock went to the north because it looked as white as winter, and winters always came down from the north. The black rock reminded him of a meteorite, even though it was earthly, and Ray remembered seeing shooting stars coming from the east. The gray rock seemed to belong in the south to him, so that was where he placed it. The three quartz crystals all went in the center, because the Creator used crystals to create life.

The snakeskin was for the east because it represented a new beginning, a new life. The finishing nails he'd straightened went to the north and south for the two magnetic poles, and the pine cones and seedpods were for the east, for growth. The hawk feathers, his last remaining gifts, were for the Creator, serving as flight, to see the creations.

He completed his medicine wheel.

"Thank you," he said aloud to no one in particular.

It was beginning to glow outside. The morning returned, and he immediately wondered where the stars and moon had gone. "They were j-j-just here," he said. "W-W-Weren't they? Wh-What's h-happening?"

Ray entered his third day of wakefulness.

Time zoomed by. The ball of fire began creeping over the mountains yet again.

An owl flew silently past the entryway, and he wondered if it was the same one from the other day.

It must be her, he thought. *What's she trying to tell me?*

Time seemed to pause.

Where's Billy? he wondered. *Is he ever coming back, or is that him sitting outside? And who's he with? No, those are the trickster raccoons I saw earlier, scratching around my medicine wheel. They'd better leave my gifts alone. But maybe the gifts are for them.*

Time then seemed to bend.

Does Billy need to be here to show me the way? No. I decide. But where am I going? Why am I here? I am here because I am becoming free. I am becoming part of something bigger. I am becoming one with my Creator.

Yes! I am writing my story for me, for my happiness, for all to see.

I am moving into the light, and I am bringing song—the Creator's song, my song—to the places in me that have never heard music. I can see the beautiful garden, where I have always been and will always be, where all life resides. I am walking there hand in hand with my Creator.

Suddenly, Ray sensed someone scurrying into the shed. He saw a smiling young boy at an age when everything seemed possible and when everything seemed connected. Ray had questions for the boy, but the boy ran back outside. Right then, a peculiar smell drifted from the fire, and it made Ray cough.

His body moved and swayed while he kept his eyes closed. They'd been closed for hours, but Ray was alert. Sleep was impossible—his soul took charge now, and it was tireless.

The spirits were with him now, and he spoke with them as if he'd always known them.

"Why have you called for us this time, Ray?" East carefully whispered in her soft, warm, playful voice.

"I want to know my purpose in life," he answered.

"We know what it is. You should just ask," South said, sounding composed and eager to help, as he always did.

"Yes. Ask us," North said in his booming, masculine voice.

"What is my life's purpose?" Ray asked.

"Don't tell him!" West shouted out. Her throaty, sultry drawl made her sound as though she were a bitter old woman. "That's not why he called us here, and that's not what he wants to know."

"I think West is right," South said.

"Of course I am," said West. "And I'm pretty sure he knows the answer to his foolish question anyway."

"What is it you really want, Ray?" East gently asked.

"I want to know—" He stopped.

"Yes?" East quickly said.

"I—"

"Lost boy! What do you want from us?" said West, pressing at him.

"Why are you calling me that?" Ray asked.

"What? Lost boy? You don't like that name?"

"No, I don't like it. What does it mean anyway?" he asked.

"Leave him be," North said to West. "Now is not the time."

"Whatever," West said. "Just answer the question, boy. What do you want from us?"

"I don't know," Ray said.

"You don't know?" South asked.

"Of course you do. Be strong, son," North bellowed.

Ray knew North was correct. Because more than anything, he wanted to know who the boy in his visions was and to know if he was real. But asking that question meant asking the question he'd avoided his entire life. It scared him to even think about it.

"Go on then," West said. "Ask it. Don't be a coward."

Am I really a coward? he wondered.

"If you hide behind a simple question, you certainly are a coward," North said.

"You can hear my thoughts?" Ray quickly asked.

"We hear everything. And we know everything," said East, "because we're always with you. We've always been with you."

"Then why do I need to say it if you already know?"

"Because nothing will change unless you do, Ray," the Creator said, speaking to him for the first time. "You came here for a reason, and it's time for you to show yourself and show all of us here that you are ready to take the next step in your life."

"It's OK," East said, offering comfort to him.

Ray knew he had no other choice now. He drew in strength. "I want to know who he is," he said, and he let out a long sigh of relief.

What followed was unexpected silence. Ray had hoped to hear a flow of answers, but none of the spirits said a word. He repeated his statement, this time louder. "I want to know who he is!"

"We heard you the first time," West said.

"Is that really your question, Ray?" Creator asked in her usual assuring and direct voice.

"Yes. I want to know who he is, the boy from my dreams. I want to know everything about him." Ray paused. His real question was right there, and he knew he had to ask it now. "I want to know if ..." He sobbed. "I want to know if I'm him."

"There it is," the Creator said. She cheered, and the other spirits celebrated with her, except for West.

"There is nothing to be afraid of, Ray," Creator promisingly said. "You have lived many lives before this one, and you will live many lives after."

"I have? I will?"

"Yes. Many more lives. Many more," South responded.

Ray's shoulders dropped as his head and chest sank. It was as if all of life's problems had just been stacked on top of him, pushing him down deep into his medicine wheel.

"But why is life so hard?" he asked.

"It's only hard until it isn't," South said.

"What does that mean?"

"It means you decide if you want your life to be hard or not," North said.

"I decide?"

"That's right," South said.

"I don't understand," Ray said. "When do I do that? How do I do that?"

"All of life is a choice, Ray," Creator said. "And you've chosen everything about it so far."

"I have?"

"Yes. And you can always choose something else," North said.

"I can?" he asked.

"It's your life, isn't it?" East asked.

"Yeah, but—"

"There is no *but!*" North nearly shouted. "There's only you and your choices. So what do you choose?"

I get to choose? Ray thought, though the spirits heard his words clearly.

"And whatever it is you choose," Creator said, "just remember that you can't mess it up. No matter how much you think you are, you can never mess it up. Your life is perfect. It's always been perfect."

"My life is perfect?"

"It most certainly is," Creator answered. "It's always been."

Ray took his time to think about what had been said. It didn't make any sense, yet at the same time, it made absolute sense.

"What do you choose?" West asked.

"I don't want my life to be so hard anymore," Ray said.

"That's not a choice," said West.

"It's not?"

"Not wanting something is not choosing," North said. "It's rejecting."

"Then I choose to be happy," he said.

"Then you will be," Creator said, "but you will have to make that choice every day, even on the days that seem hard."

Ray nodded. "I understand," he said.

"You say that now," said West, "but let's see what you do when death is upon you." She giggled.

"Why? What happens when we die?" he asked.

"We don't die! But you do," West said mockingly.

"I know. But what happens when I die?"

They told him.

Moments later, Ray asked about his visions. "What was his name?"

They told him.

"Where did he live?"

They told him.

Ray continued asking questions, and the spirits answered them all.

Hours went by, or so it seemed.

Soon Ray had nothing left to ask.

"He looks like he's done," North said.

"Is this true?" East asked Ray.

"Yes, I think so," he answered. "You've answered all my questions."

"Then this is good news," the Creator said. "How do you feel?"

"I don't understand your question," he said.

"She wants to know how you feel," West snapped. "It's a simple question, don't you think?"

Ray remembered just one person ever asking him that and seeming to care about his answer. But she was gone now. "I feel, well, fine, I guess," he said.

"What does *fine* feel like?" West asked, sounding irritated.

Ray didn't know.

"What feelings do you have right now, Ray?" East gently asked.

As simple a question as it seemed, the answer escaped him. "I don't know," he said.

"He's disconnected, so he isn't feeling anything," South said.

"He's never been connected," West said. "All he's ever felt is sad and sadder."

"Is that true?" Creator asked.

"It's true," he said.

"What a waste of life, not to feel all that there is," South said disappointedly.

"We all know he has feelings. He just doesn't like them, and he pushes them all away," said West. "And he doesn't even like the ones that feel good."

Ray nodded.

"He can connect with us just fine, but ask him to connect to his own body, with his own self, and he can't do it," West said.

"Why don't you help him?" Creator said to West.

"Maybe he doesn't want my help," she answered.

"Ray, would you like help in connecting to your body?" Creator asked.

"Yes, but what's going to happen? What is she going to do?"

"You're going to feel something. That much I can promise you." West snickered.

"Don't let her scare you, Ray. You can handle it. You're strong," North said.

"Are you sure?"

"Some of us here think you are, but not me," West said.

Ray considered his options and decided, *I've come this far.*

"Have you the courage to go further?" North asked.

"Of course he does," East said, trying to shelter her friend. "Right, Ray?"

"Yes."

"Well then, you need to ask West for her help," Creator said.

Without hesitation, Ray did so. "West, will you please help me to connect to my body?"

"I thought you'd never ask," she said, and she immediately blew warm air onto his face. The warmth traveled through him quickly.

"This feels good," he said, feeling relief from the brisk air.

But as the air warmed and comforted him, it started to get hotter and hotter. Suddenly, the heat turned into sharp electrical zaps, and the zaps darted at him faster and faster. They touched every nerve in his body and zapped him all at once. Thousands of zaps, probably millions, stung his whole body and face.

He screamed from the pain. "Ahhh! Make it stop! Please! Make it stop!"

"How do you feel now?" West smugly asked.

"Why are you doing this to me? Ow! Please! Please make it stop!"

"You haven't answered my question," she said.

"I feel pain! Please! Stop hurting me!"

With his last plea for help, West snapped her fingers, and everything Ray had been feeling went away immediately.

"How do you feel now?" she asked.

"Oh jeez, thank you. Thank you," Ray said to her.

"How do you feel, Ray?" Creator asked.

"I feel"—he studied his body—"relieved."

"With just a snap of my fingers," West said, "I can make it all come back. How does that make you feel?"

"That scares me," Ray said to her. "It makes me feel trapped and used. Like you're messing with me. And it makes me feel worthless, like I don't matter to you. The way I've felt my whole life!"

"And with a snap of my fingers," Creator said, "I can make her go away, and she will leave you alone forever. How does that make you feel?"

"That makes me feel"—he thought carefully about his response—"sad. Sad and empty."

"Why is that?" Creator asked.

"Because I don't want her to go away. I need her here. I want her here. I don't ever want her to leave me."

"Thank you," West said. "I'm starting to feel the same about you."

"You're welcome," Ray answered. "How do *you* feel now?"

"I feel appreciated," she said. "Do you know what that feels like, Ray?"

"I do now," he told her. "I do now."

CHAPTER 35

I t was twilight when his journey with the spirits ended.

"We're always with you," they said just before he fell into a deep sleep.

Hours later, as the afternoon fireball approached overhead, he awoke to the chirping of birds, the gentle rustling of tall grasses, and the trembling of leaves.

As he opened his eyes, Ray took careful notice of all the things around him. He looked at the shed's wood paneling, which now appeared bright brown, with hundreds of sharp dark lines that somehow had been intelligently placed. He noticed the flat burnt-orange color of the dirt floor, which had seemed so plain to him just days earlier. He stared at the coal in the pit and couldn't believe all the different shades of gray and black. Ray thought about all the logs he'd burned and how, at one time, those logs had come from tiny seeds that had grown into trees. He wondered about the lives of the trees, their ages, if they had lived nearby, and if one of them had fallen recently. He thanked them for bringing him warmth and comfort.

Ray gave thanks to everything else around him for helping him on his journey.

He sensed everything now and had a connection to it all, just like when he was a small boy.

A moment later, glimpses of his time with the spirits started coming to him.

Who were they? he wondered. *Wait! Were those really the spirits? Or was my mind playing tricks on me? No, it must've been them. Or was all of it just a dream?*

Suddenly, a woman's voice whispered in his ear. "You weren't dreaming," she said. "You asked for our help, so we came."

Ray looked around the shed, searching for her. "Who are you?" he asked aloud.

"It was all real," she whispered again.

Her words sounded like a memory to him.

"Who are you?" he asked again.

"In time, you will remember everything," she replied, "but for now, the place you are looking for is Wallace."

"W-Wallace? Wh-Where's that?" he asked.

"That is where he is from."

A chill ran up and down Ray's arms and the back of his neck. "Who?" he asked, though he already knew the answer. "Am I s-supposed to g-go there?"

She didn't answer him.

"What am I s-supposed to do?" he shouted.

A deep male voice answered, "You will go to Wallace, and you will find out everything."

"Go there, Ray," another woman said encouragingly.

"The answers are there for you," another man said. "You will see." The man's voice faded, and Ray somehow knew the others were leaving him too.

"Wait!" he shouted. "Don't g-go yet! C-Come back!"

But his pleas went unanswered.

A short time later, Ray rose to his feet and began packing up his things. "I'm g-going to W-Wallace," he said with a wondrous look on his face.

After his long, quiet hike back, Ray saw the shaman standing at a barbecue grill and swiping at smoke blowing toward his face. Somewhere behind the white cloud, Ray recognized Eddie sitting in a lawn chair. At that moment, a big grin spread across Ray's face, and his eyes brightened like the sky above.

As he walked closer, he could smell what the shaman was grilling. He quickened his steps.

Before long, Ray was embraced in a long and solid hug with the shaman and then with Eddie.

"Welcome back," the shaman said.

"Th-Thanks," he replied. "Th-Thanks for everyth-thing."

"How do you feel?" the shaman asked him.

Ray knew exactly how he felt. "I f-f-feel hungry," he said, and he smiled while he rubbed his empty stomach.

For the rest of the afternoon, Ray sat and laughed as he listened to stories told by Eddie and the shaman. The whole time, neither of his friends asked what had happened to him in the shed.

Ray understood why. *That time belongs to me.*

The sun started to set, and they moved the gathering inside the house, to the kitchen table. It was then that Ray followed his urge to tell them what he'd wanted to since leaving the shed.

"I'm g-g-going to W-Wallace," he said.

CHAPTER 36

"I'm g-going to f-find the p-place from my d-dreams," he said. "It's c-called W-Wallace."

"Do you know where it is?" the shaman asked.

"No, n-not y-yet."

The shaman got up from his chair and hurried toward his bedroom. "I'll be right back!" he shouted from down the hallway. A moment later, he returned, carrying a laptop computer. "Here. You're probably better at this than I am," he said to Ray while handing it to him.

The three of them crowded around the computer.

"Well," Ray said while counting the names on the screen, "th-there're a l-lot of cities with th-that name."

Eddie and the shaman inched even closer.

"There's one in California," the shaman said, and he pointed to the link, almost touching it. "Let's look at that one."

Ray moved the pointer.

"It's not too far from here," the shaman said. "Just a couple hours away."

The young man clicked on the photos of Wallace, California.

"Does it look familiar?" the shaman asked.

"No," Ray said while he continued his search. It took him just another minute to make his conclusion. "That's n-not it," he told them.

"You're sure?" the shaman asked.

Ray nodded.

"Go to the next one, in Idaho," the shaman said.

"I'll d-d-do it later," Ray said as he began sniffing the air around him.

"Not now?" the shaman asked.

"No. I n-n-need to t-t-take a shower."

Later that night, after Eddie had gone home, Ray sat in the living room and continued his search on the computer. The shaman sat close by.

The next city on the list was Wallace, Idaho. It was a mining town surrounded by the Bitterroot Mountains. Ray dismissed that city right away. Next was Wallace, Indiana, and that one took him a little longer to rule out.

The next city named Wallace was in western Kansas. It had a tiny downtown with several brick buildings and was surrounded by farmland everywhere, for hundreds of miles in all directions.

"You found it," West said softly in his ear.

"I f-f-found it," he excitedly said to the shaman. "This is it."

"You're sure?"

"I'm s-sure." He rapidly clicked through the photos.

"Now what?" the shaman asked.

"I have to g-get there," he said.

CHAPTER 37

A calm and clear announcement sounded over the loudspeaker and echoed across the marble floor of the train station: "Now arriving."

"Will you t-t-tell Eddie what I'm d-d-doing?" Ray asked the shaman.

"Of course."

"And I'll c-c-call you when I c-c-can," he said.

"I'd rather hear from you in person," the shaman answered. "If you don't mind."

"What if it t-t-takes me a l-l-long time to c-c-come back?"

"Then I'll wait," the shaman said.

"Then I'll c-come back. I p-p-promise."

A loud earthly rumble then interrupted them, as did the eager passengers rushing to the boarding area.

As Ray was about to say goodbye, the shaman asked him to promise him something else. "Don't stop until you're done. Until you have all your answers. Can you do that for me?"

"I p-p-promise," Ray said, and he reached out his hand to give his friend a firm handshake, as men did. Right afterward, they embraced in a long, careful hug, as real friends did.

"Wait," the shaman said. "I almost forgot. I have something for you." He reached into his pants pocket and pulled out a folded stack of hundred-dollar bills. "You might need this." He held it out for Ray to grab hold.

"Wh-What's this?" Ray asked while his eyes locked on the largest amount of money he'd ever seen.

"It's something you might need to keep your promise to me."

"B-But I d-don't—"

"Don't worry about where this came from. I earned this just for you," the shaman said.

Ray noticed a smirk on his friend's face. "What d-do you m-mean?" he asked.

"I'll tell you when you get back, and then we'll both have stories to tell," the shaman answered, and he forced the cash into Ray's hand. "So until we meet again."

"We will. I p-p-promise."

Minutes later, the train began rolling east along the tracks.

The following morning, Ray disembarked in Lamar, Colorado. Wallace, Kansas, was now just a hundred miles away. His plan was to walk all the way there if he had to, though he hoped to find another way.

Once he got to Wallace, Ray had no idea what he'd do next.

CHAPTER 38

Richard Tanner owned two pairs of denim overalls; he'd bought them both at the same time when they were on sale nearly twenty years ago. One of the pairs he used for work, and the other he kept as his spare. The spare hung in his closet with the tags still on them.

Richard was eighty-two years old, and he appeared his age. He had a full beard that was white and short, and it matched the sides of his otherwise bald head. His face was wrinkly and rough, and his deep blue eyes seemed hidden behind decades of hard work. He had a rugged upper body, with thick forearms and broad shoulders, and his big belly hung over his slight waist.

Despite his age, Richard usually worked a full day on the farm, the farm his family had owned for generations.

"I'm still doing my part," he often told his wife of more than fifty years on mornings when she tried to get him to take the day off.

"Suit yourself," she'd say.

But this morning, Richard had decided to stay in bed a little longer than usual. He told his wife, Judy, that he felt a little under the weather.

"Need me to fix you some soup?" she asked while pressing the back of her wrinkled hand against his forehead.

"Maybe for dinner, if you don't mind."

"Well, I do mind, but I'll make it anyway," Judy said, slowly sliding her hand back and forth along his brow. "You don't have a fever, but just stay in bed anyway, and come out for breakfast when you're ready."

"Yeah, I think I'll do that," Richard said, and he rolled over onto his side and pretended to go back to sleep.

"So where's Dad?" Mitchell asked, entering the kitchen and seeing his father's empty chair.

"He's still in bed," Judy answered while standing at the sink, "and he'll be there for a while."

"Is everything OK, Mom?" he asked, making his way to the country stove to pour himself some coffee. Mitchell walked over to the table and filled his wife's half-empty cup.

Mitchell Tanner was the only child of Richard and Judy. He and his wife, Roberta, had recently moved back home to help take care of his parents and continue running the family farm.

"He's fine," Judy said. "Today's his brother's birthday, and he always gets to feeling this way."

"He does?" Mitchell asked.

"Yep, he sure does," Judy said, "but he usually comes out of it by noon."

"Should we do anything?" Roberta asked, turning toward Judy.

"No. I don't want him thinking I know what he's up to."

"I didn't think Dad knew how to get sad," Mitchell said.

"Your father would never call it that, Mitchell. He'd say he was just remembering."

Richard had been just fourteen years old when his older brother, Charley, didn't come home one day. Charley had been eighteen at the time.

Charley was always exploring the Great Plains, and he often took Richard with him when he went on hikes. But on one particular trip, Charley said he wanted to be alone.

After Charley went missing, Richard held out hope that he'd see him again. He'd often sneak away to go searching for him, usually to where Charley had said he'd be going the day he went missing. But mostly, Richard would just sit alone on the porch steps for hours and stare out at the horizon, expecting to see his big brother walk up the driveway.

Richard and Charley had a special bond that few brothers had, and Richard trusted him like no other. He loved his brother very much but had never learned how to say it.

His father often told him he needed to accept what had happened, and he even showed him Charley's death certificate. But that only seemed to create a bigger divide between the father and son, a divide that was never mended.

Late in Richard's adult life, he finally let go of his childhood belief, but by then, he had grown to regret having never told his brother how much he loved him.

Through the years, Richard lived with an ache deep inside him, an emptiness that couldn't be filled, not even by his family.

As Richard lay in bed that morning, pretending to sleep, he thought about Charley's birthday celebrations and how he always had made a big deal about it. He remembered his brother waking up early to decorate the house just the way he wanted it. He'd move furniture around, turn chairs upside down, and build a fort for them in the living room, where they'd spend the night.

It was the best part of Richard's life—but all that fun disappeared when Charley did. The summer months soon became a time Richard despised, and the rest of the year was no different.

Richard remembered his brother's whooping laugh and how infectious it was. He remembered how smart Charley was, like always knowing which fishing bait to use in the morning and which to use at sunset. He remembered how his brother could make fires without using matches and knew so much about the tribes who lived on the plains.

But mostly, Richard remembered how much he missed his big brother, even to this day.

Not long after, Richard stopped his remembering and got out of bed.

"Oh, good morning, Richard. How are you feeling?" his daughter-in-law asked as he entered the kitchen.

Richard sat down at the kitchen table without saying a word. A plate of cold scrambled eggs and slices of bacon waited for him.

"I heard you woke up feeling a little under the weather," Roberta added.

"I'm fine," Richard grumbled.

Roberta glanced over to Judy, and they gave each other a look as if they were schoolgirls in on a secret.

"Are you fine enough to do your dishes when you're done?" Judy asked. "Because I've got other things to do than to clean up after you all day."

"I can take care—"

Richard interrupted Roberta. "I'll do it," he said, practically shouting. "You two just get on with your day and leave me be."

"That's fine by me," Judy said, and she dried off her last dish with a towel and placed it in the cabinet just above her head. She walked out of the kitchen with Roberta following a few steps behind.

A little while later, Richard Tanner stood at the sink, casually scrubbing his plates. Hot water ran over his rough hands. It had been a long time since he washed the dishes, and he enjoyed the sensation of the water flowing between his sausage-sized fingers.

As he relaxed into his chore, he looked out the window and stared at the giant oak tree that had always stood nearby.

That tree was old when I was little, Richard thought. *Maybe two hundred years old, if I had to guess.*

Then, suddenly, like a dust devil that arrived without warning, Richard recalled a summer day with his brother underneath the oak. They were drinking soda pop and eating crackling pork rinds, their favorite snack. In the fast-moving memory, Charley was telling Richard stories of what it meant to pass on.

"I'm telling ya, this ain't the only life you live," Charley said.

"Mama said not to tell me things like that," Richard whispered back.

"But she's not here, Goose."

"Mama said not to call me that anymore. She thinks you're just making fun of me."

"Aw, c'mon. You know I'm not doing that."

"I know. But if Mama found out why you call me that, she'd have Papa give us both a whoopin'."

"I'll tell you what. I'll just call you Goose when it's just you and me around, and Mama won't have to hear me say it. How does that sound?" Charley asked, and he reached out his hand to seal the agreement.

Richard hesitated while he considered his options.

"So we have ourselves a deal then?"

"OK," Richard said, and the two brothers shook hands as gentlemen did.

"Now, let me finish my story."

"It sounds scary."

"No, Goose, I'm just telling ya what I think happens when we die."

"I don't think I'm going to like this," Richard said. He grabbed hold of his bottle of cola and took a drink.

Charley leaned closer. "I think you come back as someone else."

"Do you mean like a ghost?"

"No, silly. You come back as another person."

"Why?"

"I don't know why. You just do. You come back. And you do it again and again."

"How many times?"

"I don't know. Forever, I think."

"How do you know?"

"I don't know how I know, Richard. I just do. And I'm telling ya,

I've done this before, and I'll do it again. I'm coming back—that's for sure."

Richard smiled—his brother had just called him by his first name.

"I'm a lot older than you, so I'm pretty sure I'm going to die first. So I promise you that when I do die, I'm going to come back and visit you."

"You will?"

"Sure I will. You want me to, don't ya?"

"Yeah."

"Well, OK then. I promise you right here and right now. I'm a man of my word, and I promise you I'm coming back to see you."

Charley held out his hand again, and Richard grabbed hold. They shook hands once more but this time like two farmers at the end of a peaceful negotiation.

"But if you come back to see me as someone else, how am I gonna know it's you?"

"You see, now, that's a good question, Goose. I'm not really sure about that part. I think you're going to have to test me or somethin'."

"What do you mean, like ask you questions?"

"Yeah. Let's say you meet someone who says he's me; you're gonna have to test him—you know, ask him questions that only you and I know the answer to."

"What questions should I ask?"

"Well, let's think about that," Charley said. He took a big sip from his soda bottle, swallowed, and let out an "Aah." He said, "What's the one thing that only you and I know the answer to?"

Richard thought hard but just shook his head.

"I know!" Charley said. "You can ask him why I call you Goose, Goose."

CHAPTER 39

"Where ya headed?" the driver asked after he pulled his white Suburban to the side of the road and stopped alongside the hitchhiker.

"W-Wallace," the hitchhiker told the driver. "In K-Kansas."

"We can't take you that far, but we'll get you close."

"OK," the hitchhiker said timidly.

"Hop in. You can just throw your pack behind the backseat," the driver said. He then instructed his two children to make room for their passenger. "That's Jimmy and Jenny back there," he said to the hitchhiker. "And this is my wife, Emma, and I'm Glenn."

"I'm Ray."

"Have you been out here long?" Emma asked, twisting in her seat to face Ray.

"No. N-N-Not long," he said, guessing he'd been walking for more than an hour since getting off the train.

"Where're you from?" she asked.

"C-C-California," he said.

"Oh my. So what brings you out this way?"

"I'm l-l-looking, um, for f-f-family," he responded.

"You're looking for them?" she asked, sounding confused.

"No. I m-m-mean I'm l-looking to see where they were f-f-from."

"Oh. Like retracing your family's roots or something?"

"Yes, ma'am."

"Oh wow. That sounds so interesting," she said, and she turned to her husband and asked, "Are you hearing this, honey?"

"I sure am," Glenn answered.

"I think it's wonderful that you're doing this. And you're out here all by yourself, huh?"

"Yes, ma'am."

"So tell me about back home. You must have wonderful, trusting parents if they're letting you come here alone."

"Um, it's j-j-just m-me and m-my mom."

"Oh. But I bet she loves you dearly, a nice young man like yourself."

Ray wanted to say she didn't love him, because that was how it always seemed. But as he considered his answer more, a warmer response arrived. "I th-think she d-does," he said. "In her own w-w-way."

"That's right. We all show our love differently," Emma said. "And we never stop. We just never stop loving our children, no matter what happens."

Ray held her words for the remainder of the drive, and strangely, what she'd said made him start to miss his parents. He wondered if they were missing him too.

Thirty minutes later, the white Suburban pulled off to the side of the road.

"Good luck to you, Ray," Glenn said while bending his head to look out the passenger-side window. His kids shouted their good-byes too.

"Thank you," Ray said to them, and he lifted his backpack and adjusted it around his shoulders.

"Have you called her to let her know you're OK?" Emma asked through the open window while she reached out her hand to grab hold of his.

Ray's face lit up while he held Emma's gentle hand. It reminded him of the times he'd spent with his grandmother. "C-Called who?" he asked.

"Your mom. Have you called her today?"

He shook his head.

"Oh dear," Emma said. "I'd be worried sick every day if I didn't hear from one of them." She turned back to look at her children. "I think you should call her, Ray."

"I w-w-will," he lied.

"Oh, good. I know she'd appreciate that," Emma said while giving him a smile. "Well, you take care now. It was so nice meeting you, and good luck with your family tree project. I hope you find what you're looking for."

"Thanks," Ray said while waving goodbye.

The Suburban moved westward on Highway 96, and he watched it until it eventually disappeared. He held a smile the whole time, reminiscing about his first hitchhiking trip yet struggling with the guilt that poked and chewed at him for the lies he'd told.

It didn't take Ray long to arrive at an empty two-lane highway. He was heading north this time, on Highway 27. Thoughts of his father swirled in his mind. He decided it had been too long to keep him worrying, and he promised himself he'd call him the next chance he got.

Ray caught his next ride an hour or so into his walk. An older gentleman wearing a black cowboy hat and listening to talk radio pulled his truck alongside him.

"Where you headed?" the driver asked.

"W-Wallace," Ray said.

"I'm going right by it," the driver said. "Hop in." In less than a minute, the two of them were on the road. "Whatcha doing in Wallace? You have family there or something?"

"No, sir," he answered, shaking his head. "Just searching for something."

"Searching, huh?"

"Yes, sir."

An awkward quiet lingered between them.

The driver asked, "First time there?"

"Yes, sir."

"Well, it shouldn't take us long to get there."

Ray heard a whisper in his ear. It sounded like a woman's voice. "You're almost there," West said.

"Wh-What's it l-l-like?" he asked the driver.

"Like most places around here, I suppose," the driver said. "But I can't say for sure. I've only ever driven past it."

Ray looked out his side window and saw farmland for miles. The endless rows of wheat, corn, and grazing land occupied his thoughts while the driver spoke about life in Kansas.

The driver turned the truck onto Highway 40. Minutes later, he pulled off to the side and parked along the shoulder. "There's your town," he told Ray, using his chin to point the way. "There's Wallace."

Standing alone on the road, Ray looked around in all directions and then directly toward Wallace. Suddenly, a familiar sensation came over him. He worried about returning, as though he had stepped off his school bus and was about to walk home.

CHAPTER 40

For a long while, Ray stared at the grain storage silos just across the way. He knew the city was just beyond the concrete towers.

He sniffed at the air and smelled the secrets the acres of golden wheat and sweet corn held. He felt the fine Kansas dust collecting on his skin.

He remembered.

The sun shone brightly; it was now close to noon.

He crossed the highway and started walking down Second Street. Slowly, he wound his way until he crossed the railroad tracks. He could see the faraway buildings. He started to feel unease.

It didn't take him long to make his way downtown. Once there, though, he came upon several abandoned buildings with windows boarded up and thick padlocks securing the front doors. He saw empty lots too, with cement foundations that had weeds growing between the cracks.

Except for a distant barking dog, it was ghostly quiet. As he looked around more at the seemingly abandoned town, an unexpected sorrow came upon him.

Ray pushed the feeling aside and continued down Second Street, to where his memories took him. He came upon an old, seemingly renovated brick building and stopped in front of it. Above the door, in cement block letters, was the word *Bank*. It was just as he remembered. He smiled.

He continued his walk until he reached Main Street. *Turn right,* he said to himself, and he started down a barren road. A couple of miles into his walk, the road turned empty, with nothing but farmland around him. A bit farther on, something coming toward him caught his attention. A speeding truck was pulling a cloud of dust, and he watched as the truck came to a stop right next to him, with the dust cloud continuing to move over him.

"You lost?" the driver asked after he rolled down the window.

"No, sir," he said while swatting away the dirt drifting by his face.

"There ain't nothing up this road, you know," the driver said. "You probably want to head back to the highway."

"I'm OK, s-sir."

"You're sure now? Where're you headed?" the driver asked while looking Ray up and down.

"N-Nowhere. I'm j-j-just on a w-walk."

"If you want, I can give you a ride back to the highway."

"No, th-thanks," he said, and he backed away from the truck.

Several sharp glances later, the driver said, "Suit yourself," and he rolled up his window and stepped on the gas.

Ray moved away from the swirl, when suddenly, he heard a woman's voice whisper to him in his mind again.

Trust, she said.

Two miles and two turns later, Ray came to another intersection. He spotted a rusted, shotgun-holed street sign that reminded him he was close.

Then, less than a mile down the road, he came upon a long white wooden fence with an empty water ditch beside it.

He used to jump over this ditch, Ray remembered. *And he caught frogs in there too.* He looked beyond the fence, and he recognized the home from his visions.

For a long while, Ray just stared at the simple one-story farmhouse painted white, with black trim around the windows and with a porch that spanned the entirety of the front of the house. He rubbed his eyes in disbelief.

A warm breeze brushed over him. He felt his heart beating faster and his arms tightening. *You made it*, he heard her softly say to him.

Ray suddenly needed to say his prayer. He said it slowly and carefully. "I acknowledge the Great Spirit," he whispered, "the Creator of all things …"

A friendly stillness then settled in his mind. He was now ready to begin the ascent up the long, familiar dirt driveway.

When he was within fifty yards of the house, Ray heard the unmistakable creaking and slamming of a wooden screen door. An elderly man carefully made his way down the porch steps and limped toward him.

Ray slowed his stride.

The elderly man had on faded blue overalls, a red-and-white trucker hat, and a white button-down short-sleeved shirt. They both stopped their approach when they came within a few steps of each other.

"Are you lost?" the elderly man asked in a deep, throaty voice.

"No, s-sir," Ray answered.

"Then can I help you with something?"

"Well," Ray said, "I'm l-l-looking f-f-for someone."

"And who might that be?"

After a slight pause, Ray asked, "Have you l-l-lived here l-l-long, sir?"

"All my life, son. Who're you looking for?"

Ray thought carefully about what to say next. "Was th-there a w-w-woman who l-l-lived here n-n-named Ann?"

"Yeah."

"And M-M-Matthew?"

"Yeah. And who might you be?"

It's real, he thought as he took in a deep breath.

"My n-n-name is Ray, and I'm l-l-looking f-f-for—" He was nervous, and his stutter sounded more apparent.

"Are you related to those people?" the elderly man asked, interrupting.

Ray couldn't escape his deep stare. "No, sir."

"Have we met before, son? You seem familiar to me."

"No, sir. This is m-my f-f-first time here."

"And you said your name was Ray?"

"Yes, sir."

"And what's your last name?"

"It's B-B-Boyd."

The elderly man locked eyes with Ray, as if searching for something. "Well, I don't know of any family with the last name Boyd living around these parts," he said. "What's the name on your mother's side?"

Ray had to think about it before he answered.

The elderly man shook his head. "I don't know that family name neither. Who're you looking for?"

"Well, I'm n-n-not really l-looking f-f-for anyone. I'm j-j-just—" Ray cut himself off. He didn't know what to say.

After a moment of quiet, Richard asked, "Then what're you doing here?"

"I'm l-lost," Ray said, offering the only answer that now made sense to him.

"You're lost? But just a minute ago, you said you weren't. Now, which one is it?"

Ray immediately heard the questioning tone and saw how the elderly man probed at him with his eyes.

"Well?" Richard asked.

"I th-think I'm s-supposed to b-be here, sir. I'm j-j-just trying to f-f-figure s-s-something out."

"Figure what out?"

"C-Can you t-t-tell me your n-n-name, sir?"

"It's Richard. Richard Tanner. And this is my home and my farm."

It's his brother, he realized.

"N-N-Nice to m-m-meet you," Ray said, and he carefully reached out his hand. The two exchanged a quick, firm handshake.

"Yeah. Well, maybe it is," said Richard, "but I'm not so sure about that yet."

"D-D-Do you have any b-b-brothers, sir?"

"Son, I'm not telling you another thing else unless you can tell me what this is about," Richard said.

"Your b-b-brother," he said. "His f-f-friends were B-B-Boden and C-C-Cal, right?"

"Maybe. Are you related to one of them?"

"No, sir."

"Boden passed on some years back. And I haven't seen Cal since last summer," Richard said.

Ray's chest suddenly tightened. He instinctively lowered his head in honor of his friend's passing and wondered if Boden had lived a good life. "What was your b-b-brother's n-n-name, sir?"

"Son, I already—"

"P-P-Please. P-Please j-j-just tell me his n-n-name," he begged with an unmistakable cracking in his voice.

"Charley. His name was Charley."

Ray's racing heart began to slow, and the tenseness on his face suddenly turned to a smile. *It's Charley.*

"What is it?" Richard asked, and Ray slunk from the seriousness in his voice. "Do you know where he is? Did you find him or something?"

Then, amidst his worry, Ray saw a flashing image of an entrance to a cave. "A cave?" he curiously muttered under his breath.

"What's that you said?" Richard asked.

Ray didn't answer him, because he didn't hear the question. He was too busy staring into space and concentrating on the images he was seeing.

"Son, what was it that you just said?"

"I d-d-don't know, sir," Ray answered after the images vanished.

"You said something about a cave. How did you know that?"

"I'm n-not sure, sir. It was j-j-just something—"

"People don't just say that word for no reason, son. You must know something."

"I d-d-don't. I'm n-n-not sure wh-why I s-said it. I'm s-s-sorry," Ray said, and he turned from Richard and stepped toward the road.

"Hold on there," Richard said.

Slowly, Ray turned back around.

Richard moved in closer. "I'm gonna tell you something," he said. "I hardly ever talk about my brother. And not even with my own family. And these questions you're asking—I don't care for them."

Ray listened to his words.

"It's Charley's birthday today too. Did you know that?"

Ray shook his head. "No, sir."

"Yeah. I'm not liking this at all," Richard said.

"Sorry, sir."

Richard looked him up and down. "My brother died a long time ago, son. And you asking about him like you are now—well, I don't like it."

"I'm sorry, sir."

"Don't be sorry. Just don't do it."

"I—" Ray was about to tell him the truth, but fear stopped him. "I won't," he said instead.

"So what are you doing here?"

"I'm n-not sure," Ray said, and he hung his head.

"Well, it seems like you've come a long way for something. What is it? Why're ya here?"

Ray's anxiety surrounded him. His heart pounded in his chest.

"Son, what is it you want?"

Words stuck in Ray's throat, and his feet sank into the ground underneath him.

"Well, if you're not gonna say anything, I think it's time you were on your way. And I think it's best that you don't ever come back here. You got me?"

"Yes, sir," Ray said, looking deep into Richard's familial eyes. He recognized the hurt and the longing, and he sensed the elderly man's desire for closure about his brother. Ray wanted to tell him all he knew. He reached within himself for the strength and the courage, but he couldn't grasp it. *What do I do?*

He looked toward the west, begging for help. *Please help me!*

"You know," Richard said, interrupting Ray's silent pleas, "there was this woman who came by here. It was years ago. And she was supposed to be able to see things. Like she was a psychic or something. And I remember my mom took a strange liking to her. She got excited when she thought the woman could help find my brother. But as it turned out, she was just trying to make a buck. Is that why you're here? Are you trying to make some money off me?"

"No, sir."

"Then tell me what you want. And, son, don't you leave anything out."

"I d-don't think you'll b-b-believe me."

"I probably won't. But you're already here, and as far as I can tell, you ain't got nothing better to do."

A puff of wind from the west drifted by him. The words he sought had arrived.

"I have d-d-dreams—s-s-since I w-was little. And I've s-s-seen your house, and I've s-s-seen what Ch-Charley used to do with you and his f-f-friends. And I know th-things ab-bout him."

"Yeah? Like what? Do you know where he is?" Richard asked again, looking Ray squarely in the face.

"No, sir."

"Well, what do you know?"

"I know I n-n-needed to c-c-come here. To s-s-see if my d-d-dreams were real."

"Are they?"

Ray paused. "They've always b-b-been real, sir. I j-j-just d-d-didn't trust m-myself."

"So let me get this straight," Richard said. "You're telling me that you're my brother, coming back from the dead?"

"No, sir," Ray said honestly. He began to see that he wasn't Charley but that Charley might be him. Somehow, there was a difference.

"Then what are you saying?"

"I'm n-n-not sure. I th-think I'm j-j-just l-l-lost." He looked down at the ground, scraping at it with his shoe.

"You said that already. But it sounds to me like you're either some crazy kid or someone who enjoys messin' with people," Richard said.

Ray couldn't avoid his scornful look. "I'm n-n-neither," he said emphatically.

"Yeah? How do you know you're not crazy?"

"B-Because I w-w-wouldn't have m-m-met you."

They locked in a deep, quiet stare.

"I don't believe in things like this, son," Richard said, "but I'll tell you something: my brother did. And he had other ideas too. And I remember he liked telling me stories about them. My mom said he had some sorta gift, but I never knew what she meant. I just figured he made up those things just to tease me."

He had a gift too, Ray thought, and he gave Richard a warm smile. Richard gave a stone-cold look in return.

"M-Maybe I should g-g-go," Ray said, but Richard quickly interrupted before he could say more.

"My brother had this nickname for me. And he'd only say it

when it was just the two of us around. Do you know what he called me?" Richard asked.

Ray's body perked up. He immediately recalled one of his visions, in which Richard was just ten years old, and things started to change for him. He looked at Richard and smiled. Then Ray's smile quickly turned to a smirk, and he struggled to hold in his laughter.

Richard glared at him. "Yeah. I didn't think you'd know," he said, "but I liked your crazy story anyway. You had me going there for a while."

"B-But—"

"Now, why don't you just get on outta here before I do something you're not going to like?"

"B-But—"

"Are you hearing me, son? Get your ass off my property!"

"Yes, sir," Ray said, and he turned toward the road. He felt Richard's eyes burning the back of his neck.

He moved eight steps away. Nine. Ten.

"Goose!" he finally shouted out. "He c-c-called you G-Goose!"

Ray stopped walking and slowly turned to face Richard. The elderly man shuffled toward him.

"He c-c-called you G-G-Goose b-because you have a b-b-big one, sir."

As hard as Richard tried to hold it in, his eyes turned sorrowful, and his hands began to tremble. Ray suddenly felt what he saw—sadness and hardship—and the young man fought hard to hold in his emotions too.

But through it all, Ray somehow found what to say next.

"Is it still that b-b-big?" he asked Richard, and then he started chuckling.

It took him a moment, but Richard began laughing too.

The joy the two of them had been searching for all their lives arrived at that moment.

CHAPTER 41

"You want to tell me what's going on here?" Richard asked while kicking at the dirt as if he were a little boy.

"I d-don't know, sir," Ray said. "I have these d-dreams, and they used to sc-sc-scare me, b-but they d-don't anymore. And I u-u-used to ignore them, b-but I l-learned n-not to, and they b-brought me here."

"So what are you supposed to do now that you're here?"

"I d-don't know, sir."

The two of them spoke for several more minutes, with both asking the same questions but in different ways.

Left without any answers, Richard then said what felt natural to him and what any Kansas gentleman would have said when a family member dropped by unexpectedly. "What're your plans for dinner?" he asked.

"None, s-sir."

"Well, you've got one now."

"I do?"

"It's not every day someone like you comes around. And besides, it seems to me we've both got a few more things to sort out."

"Yes, s-s-sir," he said.

"But do me a favor."

"Yes, s-s-sir?"

"Let's not bring this up to my family. Do you think you can do that for me?"

"Yes, s-s-sir."

"Well then, let's head on up to the house," Richard said, and he led the way.

But as they got within a few yards of the porch steps, Ray's feet suddenly grew heavy, he became light-headed, and the short hairs on the back of his neck stood up. The image of the cave flashed before him again. He began to lose his balance and had to stop walking.

"Is everything OK?" Richard asked.

"I'm n-n-not s-s-sure," Ray answered, with the image now gone.

"Need some water or something?"

"No, s-sir," he said. Right as he said it, the image flashed before him again.

"Ray?"

"I th-think I j-j-just n-need a m-m-minute."

"You sure I can't get you anything?"

"One sec," Ray said.

"Take your time," Richard said.

Ray removed his backpack. "I th-think I'm j-just tired."

"Well, just take your time. I'm gonna head up to the house to let my wife know you'll be joining us. I'll be right back," said Richard, and he walked away.

Ray's feet began sinking into the ground. He couldn't move. Everything around him then started pixelating—the house, the barn, the trees, and all the farmland suddenly turned into a corrupted digital image.

What's happening?

Richard walked into the kitchen, where Judy and Roberta stood by the sink, staring out the window.

"Should I set another plate for dinner?" Judy asked with her eyes fixed on Ray.

"Yeah, I suppose so," Richard grumbled.

"And will he be staying the night as well?"

"I suppose so too. I'll go check on the guest room," Richard said, and he took a step toward the hallway.

"I'll take care of it," Roberta said, and she quickly wiped her hands on her apron and hurried past Richard.

"Is he lost or something?" Judy asked with her gaze still locked on the curious stranger.

"Can't say for sure."

"Well, what can you say?"

"I've never met anyone like him before. That much I can say."

"Well, can you tell me what he's doing out there? Because I've never seen anyone just standing like that before."

CHAPTER 42

The canyon wall was nearly vertical, and it was longer and taller than any he'd ever seen—the corridor appeared to go on for miles. Large bushes and small trees were all around, with jagged rocks and boulders stuck to the walls. Cut in the middle of the canyon wall was a narrow trail.

Ray saw this in a vision, but it wasn't of Charley.

He saw a native teenage boy sprinting barefoot along the canyon floor. Someone was chasing him. The boy dashed to hide behind a large sagebrush. As he crouched, he began searching for a way out. He looked up at the steep wall and noticed a trail not far away. His pursuer on horseback moved in closer. The boy lay flat on his stomach. He looked up the canyon wall again and saw three large rocks curiously aligned close together.

"Where are you, you son of a bitch?" the soldier shouted.

The vision abruptly ended.

Ray opened his eyes.

He looked over to the house, and an old woman slowly came into view. She was staring at him through a window, and he stared back. Suddenly, another vision came to him, and it was one of Charley's this time. The vision came and went faster than any before, and right after it ended, another one began.

Ray stood helpless as he saw thousands of them one after another.

All the days of Charley's life—everything he had ever done, seen, heard, or felt—Ray experienced at blinding speed.

However, Ray didn't know that two days of Charley's life were missing from the sudden download—his last two days.

◆

"Where're ya from, Ray?" Mitchell Tanner asked while dishing himself a helping of green beans onto his plate.

"C-C-California," Ray answered.

"Jeez, you're a long way from home. What brings you out here?" Mitchell asked.

"I'm s-searching—"

"He thinks his family was from around these parts," Richard said, interrupting to answer for him.

"Oh!" Judy exclaimed. "From here in Wallace?"

"He's not sure," Richard said.

"What's the name of your family?" Mitchell asked.

"The n-name?" asked Ray.

"You know, your family's last name."

"Oh. Right. Um, my last name is B-Boyd, sir."

"I never heard of any Boyd family living around here," Judy said, turning to Richard. "Have you?"

"No," Richard said.

Just then, Judy appeared to remember something. She looked at her plate and began slowly pushing food around with her fork as if searching for an answer.

"Hey, Dad, what was your brother's middle name?"

Richard continued eating, seeming to ignore the question.

"Wasn't it Boyd?" Mitchell asked.

Ray looked over at Richard, but Richard kept his steady focus on cutting the baked chicken breast with his knife and fork.

Uncomfortable moments passed. With all eyes on Richard now, he spoke. "Yep."

"Do you think it's possible, Dad?" Mitchell asked.

"Is what possible?" asked Richard.

"Your brother—would he have left and just changed his last name to Boyd?"

Ray saw Richard's face tense.

"Of course not," Richard said.

"But, Dad, don't you think it's odd that Ray's last name is Boyd, your brother's middle name was Boyd, and he's here looking for a family with that name?"

"They're just names, Mitchell."

"He was never found, though, right?" asked Mitchell.

"That's right," Richard answered.

"And isn't today his birth—"

"Mitchell!" Judy glared at him.

Richard lifted his eyes from his plate.

"I just thought that maybe he's still alive," Mitchell said cautiously.

"He's not!" Richard said roughly.

"I'm just asking, Dad."

"Watch yourself, Son," Richard warned.

"Listen to your father," Judy said.

"Yes, ma'am. I was just—"

"Something happened to him," Richard said forcefully. "He went on a hike, and he never came back. He left everything here, Mitchell. Everything!"

Richard gathered himself before speaking again. "My brother didn't just leave his family. And to even suggest that—well, it's just downright disrespectful to me. And to him."

"I know, Dad. I'm sorry."

"My brother wouldn't leave me!" Richard told everyone at the table, including himself.

"Sorry," Mitchell quietly said again.

Ray watched Roberta reach from under the table and gently grab hold of her husband's hand.

"Well now, there we have it," said Judy in a much-welcomed friendly voice, forcing a smile. "What do you say we finish up our dinner, and when we're done, I'll bring everyone out some dessert? How does that sound?"

All the heads at the table nodded, except for Richard's.

"Can I dish you up some more chicken, Ray?" Roberta asked, holding up the platter.

After the dining room table had been cleared off, Roberta showed Ray to the guest room.

"There's a fresh towel there on the bed for you," she said, pointing to the fluffy white square resting on the red-and-blue handmade comforter. "You go have yourself a nice shower. It's right across the hall."

"OK."

"Will you be needing anything else?"

"No, m-ma'am. You've d-d-done enough."

"Well, if you can think of anything, you just ask, OK?"

"I will. Th-Thank you, m-m-ma'am."

"You're welcome," she said, and she made her way out to the hall. "You have yourself a good night."

Following his shower, Ray turned off the lights in the room and crawled underneath the covers. Right away, the mattress bounced, poked, and squeaked at him as he searched for a comfortable spot. Ray smiled, remembering Charley always had done the same thing in his own bed.

I have to find him, he said to himself.

After silently saying his prayer, Ray closed his eyes and tried to sleep. But thoughts of the unforgettable day he'd just had, and the day ahead of him, kept his mind working.

I have to.

CHAPTER 43

Early the next morning, when it was still dark outside, Richard and Ray sat at the kitchen table. They were the only ones up.

Richard had just set down a breakfast plate for Ray—overeasy eggs fried in grease from the thick strips of bacon he had finished cooking just minutes earlier. Slices of sourdough toast smothered in butter were already sitting on the table.

It was the best breakfast Ray had ever had, and it was just like he remembered.

Neither of them said much while they ate.

Eventually, though, Richard asked Ray the question that had been on his mind since they met. "What do you think happens when we die?"

Ray saw the deep curiosity in Richard's eyes, a look he would have recognized from anyone. "I d-d-don't know. I j-j-just know we c-c-come back."

"My brother used to tell me that," Richard said. "And one time, he told me he had dreams that he was an Indian boy. He said the boy was always trying to show him something."

"The c-c-cave?" Ray asked.

"I think so. And I think that's why he went looking for it," Richard said, and he took a sip from his coffee cup. "You have any idea where it is?"

"No, sir."

"But I'm guessing you're going to try to find it?" Richard asked.

"Yes, s-s-sir. I h-have to."

"Can I help?"

"No, sir. I th-think I have to f-find it on m-my own."

Richard slowly nodded. "Tell me something. Does any of this make sense to you?"

"No, s-sir, b-b-but I th-think it will soon."

"I'd like you to come back if you find anything," Richard said.

"You're s-s-sure?"

"Yeah, I'm sure. It's the only way—" Richard held in the rest of his thought.

"I will c-c-come back, sir." Just then, Ray heard a *swoosh-swoosh-swoosh* sound coming from down the hall.

Richard quietly snarled, "I hate to be kicking you out like this, but I think it's best if you leave after you're finished there." He pointed at Ray's plate with his chin.

"Yes, s-sir," Ray answered.

A moment later, Judy swooshed her way into the kitchen in her loud, fluffy white slippers, wearing a pink bathrobe.

Ray quickly scooped up a forkful of eggs and shoved it into his mouth.

"Good morning," Judy sang to them while standing over Richard's right shoulder. "How's your breakfast, Ray?"

"It's g-good," he mumbled, chewing his food.

"He likes your cooking, Richard. Isn't that nice?" she said before turning toward the counters and the stovetop.

Ray watched as she eyed all the pans and utensils covered in grease and then the even bigger splatters on the floor.

She poked at Richard. "So what are we doing now?"

"We're about to say goodbye," Richard said, and he got up from his chair. He went over to the sink and turned on the faucet.

"Yes, m-m-ma'am. I'm l-l-leaving," Ray mumbled, having just shoved two more bites into his mouth.

"Where're you going?" she asked.

"I'm n-not sure," he said truthfully.

CHAPTER 44

R ay stood alone on the creaky front porch. The dawn had transitioned to morning. He heard birds chirping atop the big oak tree, and he caught the faraway crow of a rooster.

As he made his way down the steps, Ray recalled a vision of an early morning fishing trip Charley had gone on with Cal and Boden. The memory caused him to remain on the last step longer than necessary.

Twenty yards from the road, he turned back to the house to take one last look. He saw Richard standing at the kitchen window. They waved.

No more than an hour into his walk, Ray heard the faint growl of a vehicle coming from behind him. He turned to see a truck moving fast and pulling a familiar brown cloud. Then he did something that seemed natural to him, yet he'd never done it before. He pointed the tip of his thumb at the driver and swirled it, just as Charley used to.

"Where ya headed this time?" the driver asked.

Ray recognized the driver immediately; he chose his words carefully. "Wh-Where are you g-g-going?" he asked him.

The driver gave him a stare and said, "Come on. Get in."

After Ray climbed in, the driver stepped on the gas pedal to return the truck to speeding down the empty road. "So what's your name?"

"Ray."

"I'm Alvin. Alvin Johnson," he said.

Alvin had on his work uniform that morning—a pair of dark blue pants, a white pin-striped button-down short-sleeved shirt, and a blue-and-white trucker hat.

Ray immediately recalled a vision in which he and his friends hitched a ride in an old flatbed truck driven by another Mr. Johnson. He snickered at the idea that his life seemed to be repeating someone else's and wondered if it had always been that way.

"So where did ya end up last night? In someone's barn?" Alvin asked with a straight face.

"The T-T-Tanners'."

"So you know them, huh?" Alvin curiously asked.

"Sorta."

"I've known that family my whole life. They're good people." Ray agreed.

"So what is it you're doing out here? Visiting them or sumthin'?"

"Traveling. I l-l-like it here."

"You like it here? There ain't nothing out here to like," he said. "I mean, look around."

Ray turned toward the passenger-side window and looked out at all the scenic farmland, wide-open spaces, flowing crops, and picturesque farmhouses. He looked up at the colorful morning sky. *It's so beautiful*, he thought.

"I'd leave this place if I could," Alvin said, "and I'd go anywhere. Someplace bigger and nicer, where there's not a tractor in sight. But I can't because …"

Ray barely heard what Alvin said next. He was too busy remembering and was drawn to the scenes flowing past him.

"Growing up on a farm ain't for everyone," Alvin said, and he took his time to explain why.

Sooner than Ray expected, the truck pulled into the truck stop where Alvin worked as a part-time attendant. They were in a neighboring city called Sharon Springs.

"So where you off to now?" Alvin asked him.

Ray thought about the canyon wall and the dry riverbed below it. "Are th-there c-c-canyons in K-K-Kansas?" he asked.

"You bet there is," Alvin said, and in a matter of a few minutes, the newcomer to the Great Plains knew where he was going next.

CHAPTER 45

Ray walked an empty sidewalk on his way to the highway, when a teenage girl came from around a corner. She headed toward him. Her orange-and-white waitressing uniform was hard to miss, with a midthigh skirt, short sleeves, and a white apron that he imagined being tied in a bow in the back. The dress fit her perfectly, he thought, as it seemed to hug her shapely body just right.

Ray quickly decided she was the prettiest girl he had ever seen.

"Good morning," she sang to him with a warm, friendly midwestern smile.

Her greeting caught Ray off guard, so he responded only by staring.

"You comin' in?" she asked while she opened the door to her restaurant and invitingly held it for him.

"No," he said, and he embarrassedly looked away.

"Well, have yourself a wonderful day anyway," he heard her say as he quickly walked past her. But after just a few steps, he turned back around. He didn't know why, but he needed one last glimpse of her.

Ray wished he hadn't done that, though, because just as he did, he saw she was still holding the door open for him.

"Are you sure you don't want to come in with me?" she asked.

Ray nodded while forgetting to breathe. He turned back around and moved even faster.

After a few steps, he let out a big exhalation. *She's so pretty*, he thought. But as quickly as the fantasies of her entered his mind, he tried to push them away. *There's no way she'd like me. I mean, there's just no way.*

Several blocks later, when Ray's heart rate returned to normal, he stopped and turned around. There was something about the girl that he couldn't shake, as if he'd met her before.

How do I know her? he wondered.

Having made his way to the highway, Ray hitched a ride with an older couple.

"We're just on our way to our daughter's house," the driver said. "I'm Jim, and this is my wife, Andi."

"I'm Ray."

Even before he'd settled into the backseat, Andi had told Ray all about the newest addition to their family.

"We're gonna see our granddaughter. She was born just a few months ago," she said, "and she looks just like her mama. I couldn't believe my eyes when I first saw her. It's like I went back in time. You ever have that feeling, Ray?"

Almost every day, he wanted to say to her.

"Well, it just warms me up inside every time I see her," she said. "And Jimmy too. Right, Jimmy?"

"You bet," Jim said.

"Here. Have a look-see." Andi handed Ray pictures of her daughter as a baby and photos of her granddaughter from just a few weeks ago. Ray smiled when he noticed the resemblance between them.

Forty minutes later, Jim pulled the car off the highway and onto a winding dirt road. Ray saw a sign indicating his destination was five miles ahead.

"He was dropped off right here," a familiar female voice whispered to him.

Ray's throat tightened. He swallowed a couple of times to try to clear it, which made him cough.

"Is everything OK?" Andi asked, turning in her seat to face him.

Ray could barely breathe, as if he were sipping in air through a straw. His fear was choking him.

"Ray?" Andi asked with worry in her voice.

"Right here." He coughed. "P-p-please. L-Let me out," he said, struggling to speak.

"What's that?" she asked.

"P-P-Please stop." He coughed again. "I want to g-g-get out. Right here."

"But there's nothing here. We can't drop you off in the middle of nowhere."

"P-P-Please stop r-r-right here," he insisted, this time much louder.

Andi turned to her husband. "Jimmy, he says he wants to get out now."

"I can't leave you here, Ray," Jim said.

"T-Trust me!" he said, nearly shouting.

Jim hit the brakes, and the car slid to a stop.

Andi let out a shout. "Jesus! Jim!"

For a long while, Ray stood alone in the middle of the road and looked out at the open frontier.

There was no other person near him for tens of miles.

◆

The Arikaree Breaks was a long, thick crack in the earth created long ago by an ancient raging river. It was more than thirty miles long and three miles wide and was one of the most secluded and scenic places in all of Kansas.

Ray looked out at the rugged landscape, which seemed to go on forever. Green grasses and wildflowers were scattered everywhere, with not a building in sight.

The canyon from his vision could be seen far off in the distance, and he sensed it calling for him.

He followed the dirt road for several hundred yards, heading northwest, until it turned sharply west. He took off his backpack, dropped it over a barbed fence that lined the road, and squeezed his way through to the other side. He ignored all the No Trespassing signs tied to the barbed wires and resented that they were up in the first place.

Once across, he found a trail that zigzagged through the large sagebrush and prickly yucca. The canyon loomed ahead. Just then, his arms started tingling—from his shoulders to the tips of his fingers—and his stomach tightened, as though he'd been elbowed. He looked up at the bright blue sky.

"You're strong, Ray. You can do this," a deep voice said.

"You're not alone," he heard a woman say.

He moved steadily along the winding path. The canyon was farther away than it first had appeared to him, but he arrived by midafternoon.

He soon found himself hiking within the canyon, gradually climbing up the south wall.

The trail then narrowed to less than a foot wide, and he had to slide his feet to move forward. His left shoulder often scraped against the wall. Before he realized it, Ray was fifty feet above the dry riverbed below. He fought the urge to peek over the edge at the jagged rocks and deep crevices down the near-vertical drop, and he pushed away his thoughts of falling.

With each step, the trail became even trickier. Ray considered turning back. But he'd made promises he wanted to keep—quitting wasn't an option.

He looked ahead and saw that the trail continued its rise to the top of the wall, where it appeared to go safely over it. He wondered if the cave was somewhere on the other side.

Where else could it be?

Ray stepped farther. He was much higher now, and he surrendered to the urge to look down.

"Oh shit!"

He was now eighty feet high. Below him was certain death if he were to fall. He couldn't help thinking about it—slipping and smashing against the rocks and dirt.

I don't want to die, he said to himself. *I never do.*

He wondered what it would feel like to take a breath for the last time. His thoughts turned to Charley, and it dawned on him that Charley could've taken his last breath somewhere close to where he stood.

He was real, and he died, Ray thought. *He wasn't someone I imagined. He had a family who loved him and friends who loved him too.*

His heart beat faster.

No one will even know I'm missing if something happens to me right now, Ray thought. *My birth certificate won't do me any good now, except maybe to prove I used to be alive. And I'm not going to be missed, not by anyone. I could fall right now, and no one would even care.*

Ray thought of his favorite video game, *Fire When Ready*, and how his character was usually killed. He imagined moving through enemy territory, stepping along rugged terrain, with his crossbow at the ready. He pictured a Margeeg ambushing him from behind and biting down on his head. But the Margeeg never stopped there. It would then stab him through the chest with a wooden spike and celebrate its kill with a loud hiss. Ray always grimaced in frustration upon hearing that sound. But that was part of the game—an inconvenience mostly—because after he was slain, all he had to do was drink a magic elixir and wait fifteen seconds. Then presto—his character sprang back from the dead.

Ray's thoughts turned to his grandmother and all the feelings he'd been avoiding since she died. He cried out to her.

"Grandma!"

Standing alone on the edge of a cliff, he wrestled with his

impermanence. Suddenly, a gentle wind blew in from the west, touching him softly against his cheek.

"How do you feel?" she asked him.

"I'm afraid," he answered.

"What do you fear?"

"I'm t-t-tired of always b-b-being alone, and I d-don't want to d-die out here all b-by myself!" Ray shouted.

"Everyone dies alone," she told him.

"I d-don't want to d-die! I n-never want t-to die!"

He heard a rustling in his mind—a memory. *You have lived many lives before this life*, he remembered someone telling him. *And you will live many lives after.*

The gentle wind drifted away.

I can do this, he thought as he looked at the trail again. He guessed it to be just twenty more yards to where it safely crested. "I can d-do this," he said aloud. *One step at a time.*

He slid his feet a bit more. But the trail continually became more difficult. Ray now had to turn his body sideways to move forward. His backpack scraped against the stones and roots jutting from the wall. He slid his steps inches at a time.

After just a few more steps, Ray stopped. The trail seemed to be impassable now.

"Keep going," West said.

"No," he said.

"Don't be afraid," North bellowed.

"I am af-fraid!"

"You have nothing to fear. We are here with you," said Creator.

"Who is?"

"We've always been with you," they all said.

"Who? Who are you?" he demanded.

"Trust us," Ray heard them say.

A moment later, he slid his feet a bit farther.

He ducked under a large tree root sticking out of the wall.

"Grab it! Grab it now!" a woman shouted at him.

Ray reached for the thick root with both hands and wrapped them around it. Right as he did, the trail at his feet quietly crumbled down the canyon. His body dangled, and his thirty-pound backpack weighed him down. His hands began to slip, and he struggled to keep his grip.

Ray held his life in his own hands.

"No! I d-don't want to die!" he cried out. He kicked his legs wildly to get his footing, but his feet kept scraping air. "Help!" he shouted, even though he knew his pleas would be unheard. "Help me!"

Time seemed to stand still.

"Grandma!" he cried out.

"You can let go now," Creator whispered to him.

"No!" he cried out.

"You are not going to die, Ray. Not today. Just let go," she said softly.

"I'm af-f-fraid!" he said.

"I promise. You will not die today."

"No!"

"Trust," she said.

The word echoed in his mind. *Trust*, he said to himself.

Ray closed his eyes, inhaled a deep breath, and let go.

He dropped.

His backpack immediately smashed against the canyon wall. His butt and legs scraped at the earth. He pulled his knees close to his chest as if sliding down a vertical chute, and he sped at near freefall speed.

Seconds later, Ray crashed into the soft and sandy bottom and tumbled several times before coming to a stop and landing safely on his back.

He lay there for minutes, helpless, like an upturned turtle.

Eventually, he rolled onto his side and got to his hands and knees. He wiped at the tears trickling down his face.

"Yeah!" he screamed. "Hell yeah!"

Ray removed his pack and cleaned himself off. The scrapes on his arms and back stung momentarily as he picked at the rocks and fragments still stuck to him. He was unharmed otherwise and had made it down alive, precisely as he had been promised.

"Thank you," he said.

As he continued to gather himself, Ray sensed something nearby summoning him. He got down on his stomach and looked up toward the canyon wall. Three peculiar-looking perched stone pillars suddenly came into view. They looked as though they'd been placed in an exact formation—a nearly flat triangle—and could only be seen from a precise angle.

A small black hole lay hidden just beyond the stones.

Ray found the entrance to the cave.

An image rushed into his mind. He saw Charley smashing down the cliff and then crashing into the unmovable stones, the three guardians of the cave. Charley then dragged his broken body just a couple of yards to enter.

Ray got to his feet and began the steady climb back up the cliff.

The entrance was small—three feet wide and four feet high. He crouched his way in.

It was dark inside, but his eyes eventually made the adjustment. He reached into his backpack and found his flashlight. He looked around the hollowed space and immediately noticed it was perfectly round, as if it had been cut by a machine. It appeared the size of a large living room, twice as big as the one back at home, with tall ceilings.

Someone made this, he immediately thought.

He looked up to see two small openings about the size of milk crates high up the walls above the entrance. Faint beams of the afternoon sunlight shone through.

There was a small fire pit made of river rocks that sat near the center of the cave. Ray walked closer to it and saw a pile of ashes. He looked them over briefly until something on the walls caught his attention. He pointed his flashlight.

He noticed images made with red, black, and white colors painted on the flat, smooth walls. It was a picture story of strange-looking people, and it encircled the cave.

He shone his flashlight into a far corner. He froze after what he spotted. He hoped it was a misplaced rock from the fire pit, but as his eyes focused in, he knew—it was Charley.

Ray's flashlight hit the ground.

◆

Charley's wounds were horrific. It was a miracle he had even survived the fall, let alone found the strength to make it inside the cave. But not long after he'd crawled to shelter, he'd fallen into a deep sleep. When he'd awakened a day later, he had weakened to the point he could hardly move. Knowing his water and supplies were lost somewhere along the cliff, Charley had realized he had little chance of making it out of there.

The next morning, Charley had heard shouting just outside the cave. He'd recognized his little brother calling for him. Charley had heard Cal's and Boden's voices too, along with the voices of their parents. He had sadly listened to the cries of his mother and father begging for him to respond. He'd tried calling out to them, but his weakened voice had been too shallow to be heard.

Sometime later that night, Charley had peacefully taken his last breath on earth. But before he had, he somehow had found the strength to say goodbye to his family by writing them a note. Charley had always carried with him a small leather journal in his pocket, and the last thing he'd written in it had been a few scribbled words to his family.

Ray watched him do all this; it came to him in a vision.

After the vision ended, he picked up his flashlight and walked over to Charley's remains. Ray's flashlight spotted Charley's arm and something in his hand. He went over to it and knelt beside it. He saw Charley's journal and gently pulled it away from the former owner's grasp. As careful as he tried to be, the finger bones broke away.

"Sorry," he said.

Ray opened the journal to the page of Charley's last entry: "Will start other life soon. I will look for you. Love."

Curious, Ray turned to the first page of Charley's journal, dated February 1, almost four years before Charley had died.

> Something strange is happening. I had another dream today, but I wasn't asleep. I was hiding from Richard in the barn, when it seemed like I went somewhere. I dreamed I was an Indian boy, and I was alone, walking along a trail. I was going somewhere.

He turned to another page, dated March 15: "And a soldier was riding a horse, and he was chasing me, and he had a gun pointed at me."

He went to one of the last journal entries, dated May 30: "I'm going searching for the cave this weekend. I think I know where it is. I've seen it several times now."

The cave darkened.

The evening had snuck up on Ray, and he was reminded of his vision quest, when the days and nights had seemed to interchange without notice. With his decision to spend the night already made, he went outside to gather wood. It took him a long while, but he found enough thick, dry branches to last the night.

The flames illuminated the cave.

He took out his food supplies from his pack and set them on the cave floor. He ate slowly, and while he did, he stared at the paintings on the wall of the unusual picture story he knew he'd seen before.

He needed to figure it out.

He began looking at it from all angles—close and then far away. He got down on his stomach and looked at it from the ground. He even tried eyeing it from on his back. The puzzle proved to be unsolvable, like some sort of unbreakable code.

"What is this d-damn thing?"

The paintings were of several people, but Ray couldn't tell if they were men or women. He assumed their gender didn't matter. In the first scene, just to the left of the cave's entrance, four people stood together. Their hands seemed to be reaching for one another. In the next scene, just to the left, the same people were next to a tunnel or a snake's mouth; they were either going into it or coming out of it—he couldn't tell. In the next scene, moving around the cave, two people appeared to be floating. One soared high up near the ceiling, next to a painting of three white balls, and the other figure appeared to be chasing him. The three white balls were nearly in a straight line, with one of them offset slightly.

As he followed the painting around the cave, the last scene showed just one person, appearing connected from the waist down to something like a giant egg. The figure seemed to be reaching for something, with its palm up.

Ray focused on the egg. Parts of it now curiously seemed to have sharp right angles. He walked over to it. He noticed a rectangle the size of a cinder block had been cut into it with paper-thin incisions. He ran his finger along the lines. It seemed like an out-of-place block of stone.

He pushed the center of it, and the stone slowly ejected from the wall as if he'd pulled the handle of a cabinet drawer. The stone was long and hollow and contained objects inside. He looked inside and began pulling them out one at a time.

The first was a straight arrow with a sharp, glassy tip and a feathered end. It appeared expertly made and lighter than it should have been. Ray set it down by his feet. He next pulled out a large bow with the bowstring still taut. It seemed unusually sturdy to him despite having no weight to it. He wondered what it was made of and guessed it was the same material used for the arrow.

He hurried to the fire and set them both down.

He returned to the drawer and found a strange, ornate cup made of clay. He examined it carefully and right away noticed the handles were situated near the rim. One of the handles had a spoonlike feature that didn't make sense to him.

He set the cup back inside.

Ray then found four identical-looking leather pouches, and by their weight, he could tell something was inside them. He pulled one out and loosened the drawstring. Inside was a white powder. He guessed it was flour or perhaps something to eat. He tied the pouch back up and then set it down next to the fire.

He searched through the drawer more but found nothing else inside.

He returned to the bow and arrow and began playing with the set. He'd never shot one before and came close to releasing the arrow inside the cave. He took them to the cave's entrance so he could shoot it outside, but it was too dark out there. He returned to the fire and set them down.

He went back to the cave walls and tried to find another hidden cabinet. His hands and fingers slid across nearly every square inch of the walls, from the floor to as high as he could reach, but he couldn't find anything.

After his long and failed search, he returned to the puzzle of the painting.

Hours later, Ray decided to give up.

"I c-can't do this," he said. "I c-can't f-figure it out!"

He suddenly heard a whisper in his mind: *You're still not good enough.* Ray hung his head as his body went numb.

"What's wr-wrong with m-me?" he asked, questioning himself the way he always used to.

After all he'd been through in his life—being raised by an addict, leaving home, going days without food or sleep, traveling halfway across the country, trusting the voices in his head, falling down a cliff, and searching for and then finding the person from his visions—he had hoped to be smiling wide and soaring in delight, knowing he'd found his way in life. Instead, Ray was weak with sadness, as if to remind him, "You're still not good enough."

"What's wr-wrong with m-me?" he asked again, and he started to cry. His words reminded him of when he'd lived at home with his mother, when he hadn't mattered.

But I do matter, he said to himself, fighting against his suffering. *I do.*

The cave became suddenly still.

"What else is there?" he yelled out to the fire. "T-Tell me every-thing, and st-stop hiding f-from me!"

When silence answered him, he asked again but this time even louder. "T-Tell me! T-Tell me wh-what you know! N-None of this m-makes any sense. This c-can't be all th-there is!"

Ray unexpectedly found his courage. "Wh-What else is there?" he screamed.

He turned toward Charley's remains. "Who are you? Why d-d-did you ch-ch-choose me? Why?"

Ray's voice got louder, and his words came faster. His heart raced with rage. He directed his anger at everyone he knew: his father, Billy, Eddie, and especially his mother.

The messiness of his life was somehow all their fault.

"Why c-can't you j-just leave me alone?"

He rushed to the cave entrance and screamed out at the dark-ened corridor. "You hear me? J-J-Just leave me alone!"

His voice echoed through the canyon. He looked up at the starry night and shouted at the universe, at all the stars and planets overhead. He peered toward the Pleiades, the seven twinkling lights that had always caught his attention. Instead of feeling his usual curiosity, he looked at it with contempt.

"I hate you too! I hate all of you!"

Desolation wrapped around him as tears ran down his face.

He returned inside the cave, and right then, the people painted on the walls came alive. He swore he heard them saying things to him and caught them laughing at him. He shouted back, demanding answers. He stalked them around the cave one by one. "What d-do you know? T-Tell me! What the f-fuck?"

A lone coyote howled outside. Ray heard it teasing him too, so he slid down to the canyon floor to chase it away. "G-Get the f-fuck out of here!" he screamed while running up and down the riverbed to search for it. It was too dark, but he threw rocks toward its laughter anyway.

The coyote ran off, but another sound caught his attention. A storm was approaching. He listened to the thunder in the distance and noticed the winds starting to pick up. Flashes of light appeared far off in the night sky. Moments later, it began to sprinkle on him.

"Why me?" he screamed. "Why?"

Out of breath, Ray trudged his way back up the cliff one heavy step at a time.

His heart pounded in his chest, his nostrils flared, and his body tightened in rage. All he wanted was to be free from his life, which no longer made sense to him. "My life f-f-fucking sucks!" he shouted while he looked down at the fire. He grabbed a large branch, smashed it against the walls, and then hurled the broken pieces into the pit. He watched the flames quickly rise.

"I j-just want to g-go home," he said before he kicked the useless leather pouch and sent it into the fire. He watched it as it quickly caught on fire.

"I j-just want to g-go home," he said again, more gently this time.

He continued to breathe deeply.

"Why me?" he asked the fire. "What's wr-wrong with me?"

Suddenly, he noticed something strange coming from out of the flames. It looked like a cloud but was formed in the shape of a mushroom. He saw another cloud developing and then another. Almost immediately, the mushroom clouds circled the perimeter of the fire pit, as if slowly chasing each other. They continued their movement until they somehow seemingly collectively decided to merge into one giant, ethereal pearl-white fog.

The fog then seemed to come alive.

It hovered and danced above the pit, often changing shape, until it had had enough. Then, without explanation, it darted at Ray. He had no time to escape; all he could do was watch as it wrapped around him.

"Help!"

He began whiffing at the horrible smell, which was like a combination of burned animal hair and human urine. He tried holding his breath, but the smoke kept encircling him, trapping him, no matter what he did or where he went. He had no choice but to inhale deeply.

Several gulps later, Ray started coughing uncontrollably. He fought the urge to vomit.

The next thing he knew, the cave collapsed on him. Without knowing how he'd gotten there, he found himself on the ground, lying on his back.

It became pitch black for him, and the total darkness appeared to be consumed by nothing. He heard silence and felt not a thing. His breathing had slowed to three or four breaths per minute, and he thought he stopped breathing altogether. His body somehow vanished. He tried to open his eyes, but they disappeared too. His soul was all that remained. He became lost within himself, wondering who he might be.

Then the darkness and the nothingness merged, and Ray wondered how that could be possible.

How can nothing become less?

Moments later, the emptiness he'd been seeing started to take shape.

Off in the distance, light-years away, a tiny white dot appeared. He concentrated on it. Something about it brought him a sense of relief, a reason to believe he was still part of something. The dot grew from the size of a pinhole to the size of a dime and then a quarter. He sensed it was alive.

Something else in the distance then caught his attention. He was amazed at what his mind saw.

Time. His mind saw time.

His mind saw the here and the there and everything in between. He tried to make sense of it but couldn't and became afraid. He wanted it to end, but he somehow knew it had just begun.

I must be dead.

Death seemed unusually comforting to him, as though he had nothing to fear. He somehow knew he would return soon to his original home.

Ray searched for clues of an afterlife. He thought about his grandmother and wondered if she was close by.

He concentrated on the white light again; it had grown to the size of a soccer ball. The light appeared different to him now, more beautiful somehow, with warmth and feeling. It vibrated and spun, moving in all directions at the same time. Within the light, he saw moving shapes—triangles, squares, and paisley patterns woven into three-dimensional cubed balls. The designs and colors moved intelligently, as if speaking a language. The light communicated with him in ways he didn't recognize but in ways he understood. It was teaching him something. It was showing him his soul. He started learning everything about himself, and Ray understood everything again for the first time.

CHAPTER 46

G anesh sat in front of his computers at Orion3 Game Laboratories
and scrolled through his software program line by line. He was
reading what he had written for level 5.003, his most recent game—a
game just for himself.

It had taken Ganesh several months to write it, more than
double the amount of time it took other programmers to write
theirs. But his third attempt at playing the level mattered to him.
He wanted his coding to be perfect because he wanted to level up.

Ganesh had already submitted his program to O3 risk management weeks earlier, and their approval had just arrived in his inbox.
"You are approved to play," it said. "Godspeed."

It was the best program he'd ever written, he thought. Something
inside him compelled him to study it again one last time before taking it to the O3 game room, loading it into the system, and pressing
the Play button.

He read the first few lines of code once more.

Introduction: Level 5.003

The boy's home will have all the essentials for sur-
vival, but it will lack everything else. Affection will
be absent; a family structure will be abysmal and
then gone. His parents won't understand him, and
he won't trust them. He won't understand or trust

anyone. He will struggle with loneliness and acceptance, and he will be in constant worry and fear. The only family member he'll feel connected to will be his grandmother, but he will rarely get to see her. He will soon befriend a neighbor, and the old man will provide him the support and direction he needs.

Volumes of code then floated on Ganesh's computer screens, scrolling quickly, while he read.

Raymond Boyd was in front of the same screens, and he was reading all the lines of code as they moved along the bending and drifting sheets of light.

Raymond somehow understood everything—each blip and flash and the thousands of dots and dashes in a language he knew was foreign to him. Raymond soon realized he was reading the story of his life, of every moment, starting with the day of his birth. Fascinated, he read through the chapters quickly, faster than any book he'd ever read.

When he got to the part that described the mysterious cave in Kansas, the screens suddenly went blank.

I was just there in that cave, and now I'm here, he thought. *Where am I?*

CHAPTER 47

Raymond lifted his eyes off the blank screens and looked around the misty fractal-patterned room. He saw he was inside an enormous computer lab, and there were countless numbers of strange-looking beings at workstations, appearing in colorful, anthropomorphic, fractal form. He knew what they were doing, because he remembered being in the room before—and doing what they were doing.

Raymond knew that the beings, the machine elves, were all there to write the script for their next human experience on earth. They were programming their next life and coding what they wanted to feel when they returned.

"I've been here before, I think," Raymond said aloud.

"Of course you have," Ganesh said.

Raymond turned around to see Ganesh, the astonishing machine elf, standing behind him. "Have you been here this whole time?" Raymond asked, mesmerized by the sight of Ganesh, the radiant being.

"I have. And I'm here to remind you of everything," the being said in an alien language that didn't use words.

"Where am I?" Raymond asked.

"It is known by many names," Ganesh said. "And you've heard it called the spirit world. But I just call it home."

"I must be dreaming," Raymond said.

"In a way, this is like a dream. And you have seen me and this place in your dreams before. Many times."

"I have?"

"Yes. But unlike those times, you are not asleep right now. And I can assure you this is all very real."

"It is?"

"Yes. And you will remember it—all of it."

Fractions of seconds zipped by, or so it seemed to Raymond, and the floating computer terminals turned back on and flashed more information for him to behold. He instantly returned to reading about growing up with his parents, Evelyn and Clay, during the loneliest times in his life.

He read about his happiest times, when he was with his grandmother and Billy and Eddie.

Everything was there for him.

When Raymond finished reading, Ganesh pulled him away from the screens.

"I want you to listen to me carefully," Ganesh said.

They were now facing each other, and Raymond stared into his eyes of eternity.

"Your life is not what you think it is," Ganesh said.

"What do you mean?" Raymond asked.

"Well, for one thing, I know it's been tough for you and probably awful at times."

Raymond nodded.

"But it was supposed to be that way," Ganesh said. "And you will soon remember why."

"My life was supposed to be hard?"

"Yes."

"Why?"

"I'll tell you in a minute."

"No. Tell me now!" Raymond said flatly.

"Well, because I wanted it that way."

CHAPTER 48

"Why would you want my life to be so hard?" Raymond asked Ganesh.

"Because I do this to win."

"To win? To win at what?"

"Your life is a game, Raymond. And I play it to win. So I can move on to the next level."

"My life is all just a game to you?"

"Yes. And it's something we've done before—thousands of times," Ganesh told him.

Ganesh then explained how he had programmed Charley Tanner, the would-be farmer from Wallace, Kansas; Hok'ee, a Native American wanderer of the Midwest; James Bernal, a homesteader from Lewistown, Pennsylvania; and Anil Bhatia, a street cook from Bombay, India, along with dozens of others.

"And the most recent one is you, Raymond Boyd."

"Me?"

"Yes, you."

"I still don't understand."

Ganesh grabbed hold of Raymond's left hand and turned it palm up. He pressed the center of it with his long middle finger and held the pressure for several long seconds.

Raymond suddenly remembered.

He remembered all the people Ganesh had just named and

others he hadn't. He recalled all their lives because he had been there with them—living as them.

"And each time we do this," Ganesh said, "the circumstances, the struggles of life, and the worries all get just a little bit harder."

"It gets harder each time?" he asked. "Why?"

"Well, for us, it does. And that's because we want it that way."

"Why? Why would you want that? I don't understand."

"I'll tell you, but I need to show you something before it gets too late," he said, and before Raymond could argue, they instantly moved to another part of the campus.

"This is what's called the game room," Ganesh said. "This is the place where the ensoulment happens. It's where the essence of what and who I am is digitized to electronic strands to combine with your human DNA code."

Raymond looked out at the seemingly endless rows of coffin-like chambers with transparent lids and studied them carefully. Lit electronic control panels were on top of them, and inside them, he saw the machine elves, the spiritual beings, lying in a catatonic state.

"And it happens right in there," Ganesh said, pointing at one of the chambers. "That's where the transfer happens."

"Transfer?" Raymond asked.

"Yes. That's where the program begins. It's where my coding is sent to embed with the DNA code of your human body—into your unborn fetus. My soul was placed in you."

"Wait—what?"

"My soul, my essence, is in you. And it was sent to you when you were just forming in your mother's womb."

"I don't understa—"

"I'm you, Raymond. And you were programmed—to be you."

"But how?"

"Information was beamed directly to you, to your receiver. It was right around the thirteenth week after you were conceived that you received the data transfer."

"I have a receiver?" Raymond asked.

"Yes." Ganesh extended his long, skinny biomechanical finger and lightly tapped the center of Raymond's forehead, his sixth chakra—his third eye.

"How is this possible?" Raymond asked as his primitive mind continued to try to make sense of the advanced technology.

Ganesh explained, "All of the programming code of who you are now was beamed straight to you before you were born. And the code runs just like it's supposed to."

"My life was already written?" Raymond said.

"That's right," said Ganesh, "but the transfer of the code isn't always perfect."

"What do you mean?"

"There's usually interference with the data. And the time of year it happens makes a difference. The month, the day, and down to the last minute."

"Why?"

"The sun affects the transfer process, and it alters the programming."

"Oh, I remember now. It's because of solar radiation, right?" Raymond asked while the knowledge steadily came back to him.

Raymond then gazed at all the chambers aligned in front of him. He saw millions of them and imagined the lives of all those spiritual beings living on earth.

"Some of them," Ganesh said, "are in there for just a few days. But others can stay for over a century. And don't forget, Raymond: our time here is different from yours there."

"It bends, doesn't it?"

"That's right."

Raymond nodded. He remembered. "Is everyone on earth right here?" he asked, scanning the endless numbers of chambers.

"No," Ganesh said. "Sometimes the transfer doesn't go through, or it gets corrupted. And for some people on earth, they have no program at all."

"What happens to them?"

"They live soulless lives," Ganesh said.

Raymond then saw a door to one of the chambers open, and a female machine elf climbed out of it. He watched as she took her time to settle into her colorful geometric form. Once she did, she clasped her hands together and then turned each hand palm up and pressed at the center. She then rushed back to the entrance of the lab. He watched as hundreds of others exited their chambers and made the same gesture with their hands.

Ganesh guided Raymond to a closed chamber. They stood over it and looked through the transparent lid.

"That looks like you in there," he said to Ganesh, pointing to the humanoid figure lying peacefully inside as if he were asleep or dead. He looked back at Ganesh.

"Yes, that is me," Ganesh answered, "and I'll be in there until our program ends a long, long time from now. After that happens, I'll rush to do this all over again."

"Sorta like when my character dies in my video games?" Raymond asked.

"Yes, precisely like that."

"My life really is a game, isn't it?"

"It's the greatest game ever created," Ganesh boasted.

"But who are you?" Raymond asked.

"I am you."

"So who am I?"

"You are a spiritual being learning to be in a human body."

"I've heard that before," Raymond said.

"Yes, I know," Ganesh replied.

"I've been in this place before," Raymond said again, but when he said it that time, he trusted his words because he remembered.

"Yes, you most definitely have."

"But how am I talking to you if you're here and I'm here and we're both in there?" he said to Ganesh, pointing at the chamber.

Raymond watched Ganesh pretend to laugh. "What you see right now is a program I wrote just for you, Raymond. Think of it as a video message to remind you—a programmed message so you don't forget."

"I'm seeing a message?"

"Yes. Like you do when you dream."

"I remember now," Raymond said.

"I knew you would."

"Will you show me what's going to happen to me—I mean to us? What's going to happen next in my life?" Raymond asked.

"Is that what you want to see?"

"Yes, of course I do."

"Well, if that's what you want, I'll show you. I'll show you everything we've written for us," Ganesh said. They instantly returned to the lab, where Ganesh brought up Raymond's program on the floating monitors. Together they read line after line of the days after Raymond found the cave. "How much do you want to know?"

"Everything."

"Everything? Are you sure?" Ganesh asked, sounding as if Raymond shouldn't know too much.

"I'm tired of surprises," Raymond said.

"I understand."

"This is going to help me, right?" Raymond asked while his eyes whizzed through each line of code.

"No, it isn't."

"What do you mean? Why not?" Raymond stopped reading.

"Because as I said, I play this game to win. And the only way I can do that is by moving on to the next level."

"Well, how do you do that?"

"The first thing *you* have to do is remember. You have to

remember that this is all just a game and that you're alive so I can play." He grabbed Raymond by the shoulders and stared deep into his eyes.

"OK, it's just a game. My life is a game for you to play. Is that it?"

"No. You must also remember that you don't have to follow any of the original algorithms I wrote for you. What you're reading right there"—Ganesh pointed at the screen—"doesn't matter anymore."

"It doesn't?"

"What I wrote—" Ganesh stopped before correcting himself. "What we wrote, for us, doesn't matter anymore."

"Why?"

"Because now you can do anything you want with your life."

CHAPTER 49

"I can do anything?"

"Yes, anything. And now you can stop believing that your life must be a certain way because of where you were born or how you were raised. It doesn't matter what you look like, Raymond, or how you talk or what anybody says or thinks about you. It never mattered."

"I really can do anything?"

"Yes. And the thing is, you've always been able to. You just didn't remember."

"I can do anything?" he asked again, still in disbelief.

"And most of all, you don't have to be afraid anymore. And you can stop worrying."

"Why do I always worry?"

"Because that's what I wanted to feel in your lifetime. I wanted you to always feel the hands of time barreling down on you as though you were spinning out of control and all life's problems were directly on your shoulders. But mostly, I wanted you to be afraid to die."

"Why?"

"I don't worry here. I don't feel anything here."

"You don't?"

"No. That's not what we can do here."

Raymond stared into Ganesh's eyes and saw the brilliant and

beautiful intelligence but also the emptiness in his existence. He remembered what South had said in the shed—that it was a "waste of life not to feel."

Raymond immediately held compassion for Ganesh. But then he realized it wasn't for Ganesh—it was for himself.

"I know it can be tough being in your human body sometimes, with all your emotions taking over," Ganesh said. "But if only you can remember what it's like not to feel anything. It's awful. And all of us here want to be in a human body so bad. We can't wait to get back."

"So if I remember those two things," Raymond said, returning to the game's rules, "we get to move on to the next level?"

"That's right," Ganesh said. "And the sooner you remember, the better. You don't want to be like everyone else and figure it out when you're just about to die."

"People remember right before they die?"

"Just moments before, yes. That's when everyone sees glimpses of this place. It's usually a bright light and a tunnel. It's part of everyone's programming. And right before they take their last breath, they also remember that they could've done so much more with their life. Anything they ever wanted. But by that time, it's too late. They pass on, and the program is over."

Raymond held a curious look.

"But you're going to remember now as a teenager," Ganesh said, "and you're going to change our programming—and then do whatever we want with our life. And then we're moving on to the next level."

Raymond thought about the rules of the game, and something seemed off to him. "If everyone sees what I see right now," he said, "then everyone should move on to the next level, right?"

"No one has ever seen what you're seeing right now," Ganesh said.

"What do you mean? Why not?"

"Well, because I'm the only one who's ever figured out a way around the rules of this game." Ganesh paused. "Try to remember—I sacrificed Charley so you can be here right now. So you—I mean we—can level up."

"I don't remember," Raymond said.

"Try," he said while he reached for Raymond's left hand again and pressed at its center.

The information slowly came to him.

"Charley was just a pawn, wasn't he?" Raymond asked.

"Yes."

"And you used him to feed me information to get me to be here right now with you."

"Yes."

"You gave him dreams and visions so he could get to the cave."

"Yes."

"And you did the same thing for me."

"I did."

"I remember."

At that moment, Raymond's eyes welled up, and his chest tightened. He wanted to cry.

"But Charley's programming is over, Raymond, and we're moving on to the next level thanks to him."

"But it's not right."

"It's what I do."

"Why?"

"I have to."

"Why?"

"I have to be perfect."

"Why?"

Ganesh ignored the question and changed the topic. "To get to the next level, you have to remember the two things I just told you. What are they?"

It was Raymond's turn to ignore, so he did.

They became locked in a stare-down.

"Why do you have to be perfect?" Raymond had to know.

"I need someone to notice me," Ganesh answered.

"Who?"

"You wouldn't understand."

"Try me," Raymond said.

Ganesh spent the next few moments explaining to Raymond who he was trying to impress and why. "It's not the same as it once was," he said. "He used to trust me and pay attention to me, but he doesn't anymore."

"Why?" Raymond asked.

"I'm not really sure," Ganesh said.

Raymond tried to find out more, but Ganesh rebuffed him.

"So tell me again," Ganesh asked. "What do you need to remember to get to the next level?"

"You said this is all just a game, and I can do whatever I want," Raymond answered.

"Good. Say it again."

"All of this is just a game, and I can do whatever I want."

"Perfect. Say it one more time."

CHAPTER 50

Raymond's body lay motionless on the dirt floor inside the cave while his soul lingered in the spirit world.

He took in a deep breath, his first in what seemed like days, and searched for his mind's connection to his body. Raymond stretched out his arms, kicked out his legs, and clenched his fingers and toes, just as a newborn did after coming into the world. He let out an uncontrollable, labored groan.

He slowly opened his eyes to see only the shadows of the fire dancing on the cave ceiling.

He closed his eyes again.

A vision quickly entered his mind.

Raymond saw a battle. Hundreds of soldiers fought with handguns and rifles against a thousand natives using bows and arrows. The fighting took place in an open area near the cave.

He saw the natives being massacred; they were outmatched by the army's weaponry. Hundreds of them were being slaughtered, and Raymond saw bullets entering bodies and blood splattering in the air.

Raymond was one of the natives in the vision. He was a young man and was sprinting for his life along the riverbed of the canyon. A soldier riding a horse was chasing him, and the soldier had a handgun pointed right at him. Raymond heard a gunshot, but he kept running. The gun blasted a second time, and Raymond fell to the ground just after the bullet blasted the right side of his stomach. He packed the wound with sand and then struggled to his knees. He hid behind a bush as his pursuer rode by.

"Where are you, you son of a bitch?" the soldier shouted while pointing his pistol in all directions of the canyon. He fired it three times into the air. "I hope you're dead!" the soldier shouted as he rode back to his troops.

Raymond saw himself, as the young native, crawl up the cliff and into the cave, where he took shelter.

The vision ended, and Raymond opened his eyes.

The walls of the cave warped back and forth, and they swirled as if he were looking through a kaleidoscope. Raymond drew in a deep breath, and the walls stopped moving. When he exhaled, the swirling continued.

As he inhaled and exhaled, the cave walls moved in and out.

Raymond held his breath and focused on the cave paintings. The picture story he had tried to figure out minutes ago finally made sense to him now. The message was right there, and it had been there all along.

Those are the spiritual beings from the lab at Orion3, and they're taking the steps of ensoulment. That's a story of rebirth, of the game. Of course!

He closed his eyes, and in the darkness, Raymond saw a colorful figure moving toward him. Startled, he opened his eyes. But the spiritual being kept approaching. He blinked several times, and each time, the spiritual being closed in. Raymond wanted to get to his feet, but he was devoid of a body. The spiritual being continued moving toward him and stopped within inches.

Raymond came face-to-face with it. They locked eyes, and he couldn't look away from the wholeness of the entity. Moments later, the spiritual being leaned away and appeared to smile wryly at Raymond. It raised its long, spindly index finger and held it for Raymond to see.

Raymond knew what that meant; he'd always known. He anticipated what was about to happen next as he held out his left hand.

The spiritual being reached for the center of Raymond's palm and pressed. Raymond's hand wrapped around Ganesh's finger.

"Remember," Ganesh said.

The lights went out, and before the count of two, Raymond fell fast asleep.

The following morning, as the sun rose over the Arikaree Breaks, four bluebirds argued nonstop outside the cave entrance. Their squabbling confused Raymond, and for a moment, he thought he was back at home, listening to his parents fighting. He wanted to fall back to sleep, but they seemed to have other plans for him. Raymond got himself together and went outside for a closer look.

He stumbled out of the dark and into the brightness of the day. The birds immediately stopped their arguing when they spotted him, and they watched his every step. Raymond located their perch and stepped closer. The two youngest birds quickly flew off, but the two older ones stayed, as they became curious about the human who had just crawled out of a hole.

Raymond watched the two anxious bluebirds fly off, and while he did, he held his hands firmly together, pressing his palms. Then, like the snap of fingers, he recalled a strange dream he'd had the night before.

There was a computer lab, he remembered. *And a weird-looking guy. He was showing me something he'd written for me. And I read it.*

He pressed his hands tighter, and a flash of everything that had happened came to him. He remembered it all.

"Holy shit!"

Unaware of what triggered the download of information, he let go of his hands. The data began disappearing. He tried to hold it in his mind, but everything was leaving him. Fortunately, Raymond managed to capture a few terabytes of data before it was gone.

The last thing he saw was an image of a computer screen with a story floating on it. He read as much of it as possible.

"No way," he said. "There's no way."

He looked over to the two curious bluebirds still perched on the branch. "It was real, wasn't it?" he asked them. Raymond then saw one of them wink at him and then turn to its friend. It chirped something quietly.

"But wait a second. I wasn't supposed to see any of that, was I?" Raymond remembered why.

"He's cheating," he told the birds. "That guy is cheating!"

He looked up at the blue northern sky and searched for the three stars aligned like a belt. It was too bright out, of course, but he somehow pinpointed their location.

"You're not supposed to cheat at this game!" Raymond shouted up at Ganesh. "You don't do that to people!"

But as his frustration climbed, he suddenly remembered how he had played *Fire When Ready* and how he had become ranked as one of the game's best players ever.

Raymond looked at the bluebirds. "I guess he's just doing what I used to do," he said. "We're using people so we can win. So we can feel better about ourselves."

Raymond gently lowered his head in shame as a blanket of guilt lay upon his shoulders. He turned to the large stones that guarded the cave, to the spot where Charley had come to a crashing halt. He imagined Charley crawling inside. He thought about Richard and how much happier his life would've been if his brother had returned home.

"It's not right," Raymond said to the birds. "And I don't care if that's what he wants to feel. He can't do things like that. We can't do whatever we want to people. We're not God."

A short while later, after he promised himself he'd play the game differently if he ever got the chance, Raymond went back inside the cave and gathered his things. He returned the bow to the wall drawer. He closed it and felt it lock. He opened and closed it again and became amazed at the ingenuity. He put the arrow in his bag, along with one of the leather pouches.

Raymond then looked around the sacred space, when a funny feeling came over him—he smiled wide. Raymond Boyd now saw death as a new beginning, not as an end.

He had found his way.

Just before he started his descent to the riverbed below, he stood beside the three stone guardians. He bowed his head, closed his eyes, and recited his prayer. He thought about Charley while he said it.

As he walked along the sandy bed toward the main road, he spotted large gray clouds off in the distance. A mist was drifting just below them, creating part of a rainbow. It was a fraction of a full arching rainbow, and Raymond noticed it seemed out of place.

He stared at it for a while, when he realized he had only ever paid attention to the full rainbows—the perfect ones, the ones that were colorful and unbroken. But at that moment, Raymond knew the one he was looking at *was* perfect.

"And so am I," he said, and he smiled.

After the rainbow had moved on, Raymond decided he'd make it a point to search for the broken ones from now on.

CHAPTER 51

Raymond found a booth by the window.
His waitress happened to be the pretty girl from the day before, and she came up to him moments after he sat down.

"Sorry, but we're just closing," she said.

"Oh, sorry," Raymond said. Embarrassed, he got up to leave.

"No, no. I was kidding you," she said with a big smile. "Don't go." She handed him a menu. "I'm actually glad you came back."

"Thanks," Raymond said, accepting the menu and sitting back down.

"So how's your day been so far?" she asked.

"Good," Raymond answered, wondering what to say next. "Yours?"

"Oh, good. You know, it's nice seeing someone here my age. It's usually just the regulars, you know?"

Raymond nodded.

"You're not from anywhere near here, are you?"

"No."

"So where're you from?"

"California," he answered while wondering why the pretty girl continued to talk to him.

"Oh, cool. What brings you to our part of Kansas?"

"Just traveling."

"Where to?"

"Well, here. But I'm not sure where I'm going next," Raymond said. He felt the sudden urge to write something. He reached into his pack to grab his journal.

"I can do anything I want," he wrote.

The girl watched him, and without Raymond noticing, she tilted her head to read what he'd written. "I'll give you another minute to decide," she said. "I'll be back."

While eating his lunch, he wrote about the vision he'd had the night before. He described the lab, the floating computers, and the rules of the game. He struggled to believe it all.

In the middle of his concentrating, his waitress returned to check on him. "Well? How's everything?" she asked.

"Good," he replied, eager to say more.

"So here's an idea for you," she said. "Since you don't know where you're going next and I'm not going anywhere, maybe we can go do something together while you're still here." She giggled.

"Um …"

"What do you think?"

"Yeah, sure," he said, though he was uncertain what he had just agreed to. He looked into her big brown eyes.

"Great," she said. "Here's my number." She handed Raymond a neatly folded piece of paper. "I'll be right back," she said, and she hurried off toward one of her other tables.

She's too pretty for me, Raymond thought. *There's no way.* He decided she was just kind to him because that was the way she treated all her customers.

He watched her glide away with her high ponytail twirling about her head. He stared at her shapely body and watched her hips shift rhythmically. At that moment, he wanted to hold her in his arms, and he wanted her to hold him back.

Raymond opened the folded piece of paper. Her name and telephone number were written on it, along with a smiley face inside a heart. He blushed as his body tingled.

I want to call her, but she's too pretty, and I'm—

He stopped himself from finishing.

He had been about to say, *I'm just not good enough*, but that no longer felt right to him. It never had.

Meanwhile, an elderly couple walked into the diner, holding hands. A breeze followed them in. An image came to Raymond. He was inside O3 and standing next to Ganesh.

"Will you show me what's going to happen to me?" he remembered asking Ganesh, his higher self.

"If that's what you want," Ganesh had said. "I can show you everything we've written."

Raymond recalled reading what was supposed to happen after he walked into the diner.

> The young woman will recognize him from the day before, and she will seem excited to see him. He will see that she is trying her hardest to get his attention, but he will doubt that any of it is real. He will continue to question anyone liking him, especially a pretty girl like her. He will talk himself out of getting to know her, and he will tuck her phone number away and pretend to forget about it, until he actually does.

But now I can do whatever I want with my life, he said to himself. *My programming doesn't matter anymore. It just doesn't matter.*

He looked around the diner. He spotted his waitress with the older couple who had just walked in. After taking their order, she looked over to Raymond and smiled. "Call me," she mouthed, bringing her hand up to her face and pointing her pinkie to her lips and her thumb to her ear.

Raymond counted to two and then waved for her to come to his booth.

"What's up?" she asked.

"My name is Raymond. Raymond Boyd," he said, and he stood to shake her hand. He held her hand longer than they both expected.

"I'm Daisy," she said softly. "Daisy Flores."

The two teenagers then looked into each other's eyes for what seemed like forever.

"You know," she said, "doesn't it seem like we've met before?"

"You feel that way too?"

Daisy nodded and smiled.

At that moment, Raymond believed his life to be perfect.

◆

"Get in dee back," the young Hispanic man sitting in the driver's seat said while he gestured with his thumb for Raymond to climb into the bed of his pickup truck.

"Thanks," Raymond said, and he hopped over the fender. He scooched his back comfortably against the rear of the cab. He looked to his left and right and imagined Cal and Boden sitting next to him.

Raymond sat peacefully for the next thirty minutes with the wind blowing onto his smiling face and thoughts of Daisy dancing in his mind.

"Thanks a lot," he said to the driver after the truck came to a stop.

"Ees no problem!" the driver shouted out the window, and they gave each other a thumbs-up salute.

A short time later, Raymond hitched another ride, and it was with someone he'd met before.

"So did you forget something at old Tanner's?" Alvin Johnson asked.

"No, sir," Raymond answered. "I found something, actually. Something that belongs to Mr. Tanner."

"I'm sure he's gonna appreciate you returning it to him then, whatever it is."

"Yeah. I'm pretty sure he's going to like it," Raymond said.

Alvin stopped his truck at the entrance of Tanner Farms.

Richard Tanner was halfway down the driveway by the time Alvin drove away.

"I wasn't sure if I'd see you again," Richard said as he reached out his hand to shake Raymond's. "Not this soon anyway."

"I was certain I'd see you again," Raymond said confidently.

"So did you find anything?" Richard asked.

I will need a lifetime to explain everything I found, Raymond thought. Silently, he took off his pack and set it on the ground. He bent down to grab something from inside.

"This is for you," he told Richard as he held out the object for the Kansas elder to take hold.

Instead of taking it in his hand, Richard just stared at it. Raymond nudged it closer.

"You found him," Richard said, looking into Raymond's eyes.

Raymond nodded.

Richard took the journal from Raymond. "Charley always had this with him," he said while moving his fingers along the edges and examining it from all angles.

"His body is resting," Raymond told him. "And I don't think he should be moved."

Richard nodded, palming the notebook as if it were a sacred Bible.

"You came close to finding him, sir. Real close. And he heard you calling for him, but he was just too weak for you to hear him."

"He's out at the Breaks, isn't he? Somewhere in one of those canyons."

"Yes, sir. Inside the cave."

"He found it, huh?" Richard asked.

"Yes, sir."

Richard looked out at the western horizon, appearing rooted in thought. "We all knew he was out there, but it didn't make any sense that we couldn't find him. It was as if he was hiding."

"He wasn't hiding. Your brother couldn't move," Raymond said.

"He must've been hurt bad," Richard said, and he opened the notebook and began thumbing through the pages. He appeared to be distracting himself from the images of his big brother suffering.

"There's a note in there that he wrote for you," Raymond said. "You should read it. You should read everything he wrote in there. He really wanted to tell you something."

"I will," Richard said.

"I think he wanted you to have this too." Raymond reached down into his pack and handed him a perfect arrow.

"Wow, this is probably worth something, ya know?" Richard said while he held it in his hand. "Are you sure you want to give it up?"

"Your brother found it, sir. Not me. He just didn't have a chance to give it to you."

Richard put his brother's journal in his pants pocket and began inspecting the arrow, looking down its shaft and guessing at its weight. All the while, he appeared to be holding in questions about it.

"I'll put this on the mantel," Richard said. "Where I've kept some of his other things."

"I bet it will look good there," Raymond said.

Richard agreed with a nod. "So what's next for you, son?"

"I'm not sure."

"I hope you're not still lost."

"No, sir. I'm far from lost now. I'm pretty sure I've found my way."

Richard lifted his eyes from the arrow and looked directly into Raymond's. He had a curious look on his face and stared at Raymond as if they'd never met.

"Say that again," Richard said.

"What part? That I'm pretty sure I've found my way?"

"Yeah, that part. It's gone," Richard said.

"What's gone?"

"You're not stuttering anymore."

"Hmm," Raymond muttered. "Well, a lot happened for me yesterday."

"It seems like a lot can happen so long as you're around," Richard said, and he smiled for the first time that day.

"It never used to be that way."

"Things change."

"They certainly do."

"It'd be a shame if you left now. Heck, there are just too many questions I have for you," Richard said.

"I've got answers," Raymond replied.

"Stay for dinner?"

"It took you long enough to ask me, Goose," Raymond said with a devilish grin.

"Well, I'm not sure I'm ready for you to call me that just yet, but I'll give you that one," Goose said.

"Charley made me say it," Raymond said.

"Really?"

"No."

As they made their way up the driveway, Raymond asked Richard, "Would it be possible if I used your phone?"

"Of course. Who're you calling?"

"I need to call my dad," he said. "And then someone I just met."

◆

"What are they doing now?" Judy asked Roberta while they stared from the kitchen window.

"It's hard to tell," Roberta answered.

"What sorta mess does that old fool have planned for us this time?"

CHAPTER 52

High above the lab floor at Orion3 Game Laboratories, standing behind the mirrored windows in the control room, was the company's chief architect, the game's original designer.

"Is that him?" she asked Angus while peering toward Ganesh and pointing in his direction.

Angus walked closer to her. "Yes," he said, "that's him."

"He's the one who went through level five on just his third try?"

"Yes, ma'am. He's also the one who did it before reaching his twenty-sixth year."

"How many have passed level five now?" she asked.

"Well, if we count you and me, that brings the total to seven."

"And I know I held the record for a while, but what was it before he just shattered it?"

"One thousand nine hundred eighty-four attempts. That was the last record."

"And you checked the systems? You're certain he hasn't tampered with anything?"

"We've done multiple tests, ma'am, and we've done a systems-wide security check too. There's nothing wrong with our systems, and nothing's been tampered with—I'm certain of it," Angus told her.

"Do you think he's had help from the outside? Maybe from one of our competitors?"

"No, ma'am. He hasn't been talking to anyone, and we haven't had any sort of breach."

"How certain are you of that?"

"We've been tracking him for the last few months, and he's as clean as they come. All he ever talks about is how he'll never play any other game."

"So what's he doing then?"

"I'm going to let Charlotte explain," he said, and he gestured for her to join them. Charlotte had been standing quietly off to the side, watching and listening. "She's been surveilling him for a few weeks now."

"Well, tell me what you found," the architect said to Charlotte.

"He's figured out a way to run a subprogram while the main program is running," Charlotte said.

"I'm sorry. Say that again?"

Charlotte looked over to Angus.

"Charlotte found a subprogram," Angus said.

"I heard what she said, Angus. I just don't understand what she means. Our systems aren't designed for that."

"That's what we thought," he said. "But—"

"Wait a second," the architect said. "How can two programs run at the same time? Didn't you put security measures in place to prevent that from happening?"

"He's figured out a way to embed the subprogram within his main program," Charlotte said. "The subprogram turns on at key moments and comes across as spiritual messages, visions, and dreams." Charlotte glanced down at the lab floor and toward Ganesh. "He's even found a way for you to be part of it, ma'am."

"Me?" the architect asked.

"Yes, ma'am. He created a version of you in a spiritual ceremony. It's quite genius, actually."

"You like that he outsmarted us, do you?"

"No, ma'am. That's not what I meant," Charlotte responded as she turned back to face her.

"You seem impressed by him," the architect said.

"It's not easy, what he did," Charlotte said while trying to hide her fascination with Ganesh, who was easily the most creative and talented programmer she'd ever come across. In the back of her mind, she wondered about the other ideas he might be hiding.

"Is he using the plant medicines? He must be," the architect said, interrupting Charlotte's thoughts.

"Yes," Angus answered. "But not in the way we designed them."

"What do you mean?"

"Well," Charlotte said, stepping in again, "he uses them to un-encrypt the subprogram—mainly to send himself a message."

"Tell me, Charlotte—how did you figure all this out?" the architect asked.

"Well," she said hesitantly, "that's what I would've done, ma'am."

"You really are impressed by him, aren't you?" the architect asked.

"Well, I, uh …" Charlotte trailed off in her loss for words.

"It's OK. So am I."

It's more than just impressive, Charlotte thought. *It's magical.* At that moment, something happened at O3 that hadn't occurred since the company first began eons ago: someone there felt affection.

The control room fell silent.

The architect let out a sigh. "I guess this means we need to shut this down now, right?"

"No, no. I don't suggest doing that. No, ma'am. We can fix it," Angus said to her.

"How quickly?"

"Charlotte thinks she can have it done in two to three weeks."

"Is that right?" she asked, looking directly at Charlotte.

"Yes, ma'am, maybe less."

"We should probably let our shareholders know about our systems error, though, right?"

"I don't suggest doing that either," Angus said.

"And why not?" she asked.

"Well, because it's not technically an error."

"What is it then?"

"I'd call it a loophole," he said, and he turned to Charlotte. They nodded in agreement.

"A loophole, huh?"

"It seems to be, yes, ma'am," Charlotte said.

The architect held on to their words for a brief time before speaking again. "Call it what you will," she said, making her way toward her office. "I want to see him in my office in five minutes."

"What do you plan to do with him?" Angus asked with Charlotte curiously looking on.

"I think I'm going to cast him out of here just like I did the last one."

"The last one was different," Angus said.

"Maybe, but going against my will comes with a price, Angus. You know that."

CHAPTER 53

M any decades after Raymond Boyd stepped out of a cave in northwestern Kansas, he sat in the living room of the shaman's house with his family gathered around him.

"I thought it was a beautiful ceremony, Raymond," his wife softly said. "Billy would've loved it."

"I thought so too," he told her.

"Where did Uncle Billy go?" their young grandson asked while sitting on his grandmother's lap and holding her hand.

"He's gone now," she said.

"But where did he go?" the young boy named Clay asked again.

"He's with his God now," Raymond said.

"Where's that?"

"Where?" Raymond asked, wondering what to say.

"I think it's time you told them," Daisy said to her husband while she looked over to him.

"Now?"

"Can you think of a better time?" she asked.

It took him a moment, but Raymond smiled in agreement. "You're right," he said.

"What is it, Dad?" his son asked.

"Your father has something he wants to tell you," Daisy said.

"This is a game," Raymond said while carefully gathering his thoughts. "Your life—it's just a game."

"You've told us that before, Dad," his daughter said.

"I know, and I want to tell you again. And I want you to really listen to me this time."

"We're listening, Dad," his children both said.

"There are clues all around you. Things that happen to you every day that may not make any sense at the time, but they're there to remind you that this is all just a game."

"What do you mean, Dad?" his daughter asked.

"It's all a game," he said again, and he got up, walked over to the window, and looked out at the beautiful view of the forest. "And you can do anything you want," he said with his back to them now. "All of you. You can do anything you want to do with your life. Anything."

"That's what you've always taught us."

"Where's Uncle Billy?" Clay blurted out. He hadn't let go of his question or of his grandmother's hand.

"He went back home." Raymond turned to answer his grandson. "It's a place we've all been to before. It's a place each of us will see again."

"Dad, what are you talking about?" asked his son.

"Your father's trying to tell you that he knows what happens to us when we die."

"How do you know, Dad?" he asked.

"I've been there."

"When?"

"The day before I met your mother. I remember it like it was yesterday."

"You're talking about heaven, Dad?" his daughter asked.

"Yeah, something like that."

"Heaven's in Kansas?" his son asked.

"For me, it was," he said.

"That's where Uncle Billy is?" young Clay asked as he looked at everyone in the room for an answer. When no one replied, the little boy searched deep in his grandmother's big brown eyes. "Grandma?"

"No, Clay. That's not what your grandpa meant," Daisy told him.

"Well, where is he?" the little boy asked, almost demanding an answer.

"Uncle Billy is no longer on earth. He's passed on, and he's now at a place—well, you can just call it home," Raymond Boyd said, and he looked up as if seeing Orion3 through the ceiling. "But he'll be returning here soon. He may already have."

"Was this all a dream, Dad?" asked his daughter.

"I used to think it was," Raymond said to her.

"Your father explains it all in his book," Daisy said to them. "Isn't that right, dear?"

"You wrote a book, Dad?" his son asked.

"I did, and it's almost finished."

"What's it about?" his daughter asked.

"What's it about?" Raymond repeated while slowly scanning the room as if looking for the right answer. "Well, it's about life and death and everything in between. It's about being in the moment and why experiencing times like these right now is the only thing that matters." Raymond paused. "Try to remember everything that's happened in your life, because each memory you have is special." He paused again. "And you should make plans for your future, but don't ever dwell on it."

Raymond fought to hold back his tears. "Just live in the moment," he said to them. "Live for right now, and appreciate every feeling you're experiencing. Even the ones you don't like very much."

Raymond then looked at each member of his family. "You are all beautiful, spiritual beings learning to be human. And you're all doing an amazing job. I am so blessed I get to experience this precious life with you."

He struggled a moment before saying, "I l-l-love you all s-so much."

Raymond began to cry.

His family went to him, and he embraced each with a tight hug.

"But I didn't want Uncle Billy to die," young Clay said. "I don't want anyone I know to die." The little boy started to cry.

Raymond Boyd gently reached for his grandson's hand and drew him away from his grandmother and into his arms. "There's nothing to be afraid of, Clay," he said to his grandson, kissing the top of his head. "Uncle Billy is on a new journey. And you will see him again. I promise."

Raymond then gave his grandson a loving cuddle and said, "Everything will be OK."

CHAPTER 54

Right after his level 5.003 game ended, Ganesh, the being from the spirit world—Raymond Boyd's higher self—climbed out of his chamber in the game room and went back to the O3 computer lab. He wanted to begin his programming for his next experience on earth, on level 6.000.

He found a seat next to his friend Max.

Max had been working for several hours before Ganesh arrived. He had planned to crawl inside a sleep pod and close his eyes, but Ganesh convinced Max to stay a little longer to keep him company.

"You being here helps me to remember how to do this," Ganesh said while he pretended to smile.

"I'll stay but just for a minute," Max said.

"So what level are you working on?" Ganesh asked his friend while waiting for his computers to boot up.

"Level 2.337."

"You programmed Richard Tanner on 2.336, right?"

"Right."

"I liked him."

"Yeah, me too. So what level are you at now?" Max asked.

Ganesh paused for a moment before answering. "I'm about to start on level 6.000."

Max stared at him as he considered what to say. "Why are you always in such a hurry?" he asked.

"What do you mean?"

"What I mean is, why are you always working so hard?"

"I need to win," Ganesh said.

"Win at what? This game?"

"Of course," Ganesh answered.

"You know," Max said, "you're the smartest programmer I've ever met."

"Thank you," Ganesh replied.

"But you're also the most foolish."

"What are you talking about?"

"You have no idea what this game is about."

"Sure I do. That's why I'm playing at the highest level right now."

Max shook his head. "That's not what this is about."

"What is it then?"

Max waited until he knew what he wanted to say. "Do you remember when you were Charley Tanner? And you dragged your body into that cave, where your programming eventually ended?"

"Of course."

"What do you remember feeling?"

"I felt sad, scared, alone, and a lot of other things. Why?"

"Well, why do you think that is?"

"Because that was the algorithm I wrote. That's what I wanted to feel," Ganesh answered.

"And I'll bet you can tell me the exact code you wrote to feel that way, right?"

"Of course I can. Would you like to see it?"

"Yeah, I would, actually."

Ganesh pulled it up on his screen, with Max moving closer to him. "It says it right there—sad, scared, alone, frightened. Which was what I felt and what I coded."

"You're still not getting it," Max said.

"Getting what?"

"What you don't get is that you can't have those feelings without experiencing something else first."

"What's that?"

"It's love, Ganesh." Max paused again before he continued. "This game isn't about winning or leveling up. The architect made it so we can experience love. That's the part you don't understand."

"I understand just fine," Ganesh said. "I understand this game better than anyone who's ever played."

"Like I said, you're the smartest programmer I've ever met, but you're not smart enough to see that life on earth isn't to be understood."

"What is it then?"

"It's to be experienced."

Ganesh looked at Max with curiosity splashing across his face.

"You should look back at your coding again," Max said, pointing at the screen, "and find the last thing Charley wrote in his journal."

"Why?"

"Just look at it."

A few seconds later, without saying another word, Max turned away and went straight to the sleep room.

Ganesh quickly searched for and found Charley's last journal entry. He then sat quietly and stared at his computer screens. He hadn't done that in years—just sitting there without researching anything or writing any code. He just sat in thought.

In time, Ganesh understood what his friend had been trying to tell him all along.

He recalled his lives as Raymond Boyd, Charley Tanner, and all the other human beings on earth he'd programmed. He saw what he'd been missing. They had been right there the whole time: moments of love.

Not long after, Ganesh decided to play his next game, level 1.000, the correct way, the way the architect had initially intended.

As he began his research, he felt a tapping on his shoulder. He turned to see a pretty young woman standing behind him.

"Are you Ganesh?" she asked.

"Yes," he said hesitantly.

"My name is Charlotte. Would you mind coming with me?"

ABOUT THE AUTHOR

A Silicon Valley fugitive, **B. David Cisneros** spent decades working in the tech and gaming industries, connecting the corporate world with his spirituality. Not a religious man, he devoted his life surfing up and down California's coastlines, searching for the perfect wave, where he always found his faith. Nowadays, David lives in the high desert, teaches at the University of Nevada, Reno, and spends his free time coaching competitive youth soccer, listening to old school rock, sipping fine tequila, and laughing with friends and family. And he's still searching for that perfect wave.